"You didn't want to feel like you were living in a barracks?" he joked.

"I was never into anything military-ish..."

"Including your dad? Or because of your dad?" he fished.

"The things that my father was more interested in than me have always just not...been my favorite things..." Clairy said diplomatically.

Quinn laughed wryly before taking a slug of his beer. "Things like me," he said. "And me not being one of your favorite things is a hell of an understatement."

That wasn't quite as true as it had been before she'd spent time with him recently. But she didn't reveal that. Realizing that she hadn't hated that time the way she'd expected to, realizing that she might have almost verged on liking it a little, was strange enough. And confusing enough. He certainly didn't need to know something seemed to be shifting in her. Especially when she didn't understand it herself and needed to sort it out.

* * *

THE CAMDENS OF MONTANA: Four military brothers falling in love in Big Sky Country!

Dear Reader,

Growing up, Clairy McKinnon hated Quinn Camden. Raised by a cold, distant career-military father, she had good reason to resent the boy who robbed her of General Mac McKinnon's attention. The boy her father viewed as the son he'd never had. Clairy couldn't possibly compete, and Quinn only compounded the alienation she felt by ridiculing young Clairy when she asked him to stay away.

Now here they are years later, Clairy fresh from a failed marriage and Quinn at a crossroads in his own life.

What can come out of airing old grudges, reexamining the past, revealing new secrets? Attraction? It doesn't seem likely.

Until it happens. But can the two of them overcome all that bad history and turn it into something a whole lot better? Keep your fingers crossed...

As always, happy reading!

Victoria Pade

The Major
Gets it Right

———

VICTORIA PADE

Recycling programs
for this product may
not exist in your area.

ISBN-13: 978-1-335-40793-1

The Major Gets it Right

Copyright © 2021 by Victoria Pade

This edition published by arrangement with Harlequin Books S.A.

For questions and comments about the quality of this book, please contact us at CustomerService@Harlequin.com.

Harlequin Enterprises ULC
22 Adelaide St. West, 40th Floor
Toronto, Ontario M5H 4E3, Canada
www.Harlequin.com

Printed in U.S.A.

Victoria Pade is a *USA TODAY* bestselling author of numerous romance novels. She has two beautiful and talented daughters—Cori and Erin—and is a native of Colorado, where she lives and writes. A devoted chocolate lover, she's in search of the perfect chocolate-chip-cookie recipe.

For information about her latest and upcoming releases, visit Victoria Pade on Facebook—she would love to hear from you.

Chapter One

"Clairy, honey, I'm here..."

"I'll be right down, Mim—I just need to put on some clothes," Clairy McKinnon answered her grandmother's announcement. Clairy was in the upstairs master bedroom of the small Victorian two-story house that was now hers.

From the time she was six until she'd left for college at eighteen, Clairy had lived in the house with her grandparents, occupying one of the other two, smaller bedrooms. When widowed eighty-year-old Mildred McKinnon decided to accept her boyfriend's invitation to move in with him, Mim—as everyone called her—had signed the house over to her sole heir just before Clairy's recent decision to return to her small hometown of Merritt, Montana.

She'd arrived from Denver late the night before—too late to disturb Mim at her new home with Harry Fergusen—so Clairy had come straight here, letting herself into the clutter of her own furniture and belongings that had arrived days ago, and the last of Mim's things yet to be moved to Dr. Harry's.

"I made some tea to ice—it's in the fridge," Clairy informed her grandmother in a voice loud enough to be heard as she pulled clothes from her unpacked suitcase on this blazingly hot June Saturday.

Mim wouldn't be staying—she'd already let Clairy know that she and Dr. Harry had to attend a wedding in Billings this afternoon. Clairy planned to use the day to finish packing her grandmother's things so they were ready for the last of the move on Sunday, then work to settle in herself with whatever time was left.

Aware that there was a limit on Mim's visit today, Clairy hurried.

Dressing purely for comfort and serviceability, she pulled on a too-big, too-many-times-washed gray sweatshirt with the sleeves cut off into ragged edges at her elbows, and a pair of faded black yoga pants spotted with ugly dots where bleach had splashed on them.

Ten minutes earlier she'd been in the shower, so her burnished copper-colored hair was still damp.

Rather than wait for it to dry, she gave her shoulder-length hair a cursory brushing and gathered it into a very lopsided topknot, which kept the thick mass of naturally wavy hair contained and out of her face, but was hardly attractive. She didn't expect to see anyone except Mim today, though, so it didn't make any difference to her.

Her entire grooming took about five minutes and it was obvious she hadn't put any effort into it when she caught sight of herself in the full-length mirror on the inside of the open closet door. But she didn't care. She was more interested in seeing Mim for the first time since Clairy's father's funeral five months ago.

"When do you need to leave for Billings?" she called to her grandmother as she went down the stairs and made a sharp left, bypassing the living room to head for the kitchen at the back of the house.

"I didn't hear that..." Mim called back.

Clairy started to repeat her question, but before she went too far, she spotted the elderly woman.

Clairy had inherited her red hair from Mim, who still wore it in a chin-length bob—minus any gray, thanks to Mim's hairdresser. Never without fashionable clothes, earrings, several necklaces and at least three rings on each hand, Mim was decked out in a fancy paisley pantsuit, full makeup and more jewelry than usual.

"Oh, you're ready to go," Clairy said. She'd assumed she'd have most of the morning with her grandmother before Mim went back to the doctor's place to change and head for Billings, which was about sixty miles south of the small town. Obviously not...

"Harry dropped me off so I could see you while he went to pick up the present. He'll come back for me after," Mim explained. "Twenty minutes or so—his cousin wanted us to have lunch and then go to the wedding together, so we're leaving early."

Clairy reminded herself that even if she didn't have long with her grandmother right now, she'd see her frequently because they'd be living only two blocks apart. So she didn't complain. She just went to the kitchen and hugged Mim hello.

Mim hugged her in return and held on tight. "I'm so glad you're home!" her grandmother said warmly.

"Me, too," Clairy said with equal enthusiasm.

It was still another moment before Mim released the hug. Then she stepped back and said, "How are you doing?"

"I'm good. Glad to have that drive from Denver behind me, glad to be home, glad all my stuff got here okay ahead of me."

"But you must be sad, too, though—divorce is sad! You don't have to put on a good face for me."

To Mim, divorce was unthinkable. A tragedy. Mim had been married a month before she'd even graduated from high school, and she'd gone through thick and thin with a military husband until the day Walter McKinnon died six years ago.

"I'm not putting anything on—I *am* good," Clairy insisted. "The marriage was… Well, it just was what it was… Now that it's over, I'm moving on—I'm doing a reset." It was something she'd said to her grandmother several times since she and Jared had separated, trying to convince Mim that she wasn't a victim. Because she wasn't.

"You had to leave so much behind, all your friends…" Mim said sympathetically.

"There weren't really any left who were just *my* friends—Jared only socialized with his own clique, so over the years I saw less and less of my pre-Jared friends. And once the split happened, I was out of his circle—his friends went back to being *just* his friends."

"The snooty—"

Clairy cut off her grandmother to give her the brighter side. "Marabeth has been my best friend all along and is still my best friend—it'll be good to live near her again, to see her more than a few times a year, the way it's been since college. So who I left behind in Denver isn't a big deal," she assured Mim.

But her grandmother continued to see the situation as tragic, despite Clairy's best efforts. "Still, seven years down the drain…"

"Better than eight. Or nine. Or ten," Clairy said to put a positive spin on that, too. Although she *was* sorry it had taken her that long to realize she'd made a mistake.

The same mistake she'd been so determined not to make, just dressed up to look different.

"And now that's it? It's all over and done with?" Mim said, as if that, at least, brought her relief after a lengthy battle.

It hadn't been lengthy or a battle, but rather than try to persuade Mim that the whole thing had gone so smoothly it was as if the marriage had never happened, she simply said, "Yes, it's all over and done with."

"And that visit Jared wanted yesterday morning before you left town? What was that for?"

Oh, Mim was not going to like this answer...

"It was sort of a walk-through so he could make sure I wasn't taking anything I shouldn't be taking—his artwork, anything from his collection of watches, his wine collection, that stuff. I wasn't taking anything, anyway, so it didn't make any difference."

Mim clenched her teeth in anger. She'd already made clear how unfair it was that Clairy was leaving the marriage with only what she'd had going into it. "And the girlfriend, who I still think he had on the side before—"

"He didn't even have a minute for me, Mim. I *know* he wouldn't have cut in to the more important use of his time with a side dish."

"Then how do you explain how fast he found this one?"

"That's how he operates—about a year after we were married he told me that he doesn't like to be single because his friends drive him crazy wanting to set him up. And he doesn't have time for it. So the minute I was out of the picture, I'm sure he looked for someone he could plug into the empty slot to avoid the setups and keep him free for what he *does* want to devote himself to. Unfortunately, my replacement doesn't know that yet. Any more than I did until later. I just feel kind of sorry for her."

Mim actually shivered with rage at that. "And why did he want your *replacement* to come along yesterday? You already met her."

"She's his fiancée now—"

"Oh, of course she is! Whirlwind Wedding Willy—three months to get you to the altar, and he'll probably have this one there even quicker."

Clairy didn't comment, hating that she'd let herself be swept off her feet and into the abbreviated courtship that had had her married to Jared so soon after they'd met. She'd let romance override common sense and better judgment. It was something she would *never* do again.

"You know I stayed in the loft when we separated while he went to try out a two-floor penthouse to see if he might want to buy it… Well, he does—"

"Because he thinks he deserves even more."

Clairy ignored the snide remark and went on with what she was saying. "He wanted Tina to see the loft before he decided whether to sell it or not now that he *has* decided to upgrade."

"Why sell it? He doesn't need the money, and now—when the time comes—he'll have a place for her to live through *their* divorce the way you lived in it through yours. That snake!" Mim said angrily.

Clairy finally accepted that nothing she was doing to ease her grandmother's anger at her ex was working, so she decided to just try reasoning with the older woman. "Please don't get upset, Mim. None of it is worth raising your blood pressure. I just want to put the whole thing behind me."

She thought Mim got the message when the elderly woman sighed elaborately. "I'm just glad you're home," she repeated at the exact moment the doorbell rang.

"Harry?" Clairy asked with a glance in the direction of the front entrance.

"It's not Harry—he's just going to honk."

"Company, then?"

"Not for me," Mim said. "Everyone knows I'm at Harry's now. Maybe it's Marabeth…"

"I don't think so… She was going to come by to help around here today. Then, just before I got in last night, she texted me that she couldn't make it and put a whole lot of giddy emojis at the end of the text—I don't know what that was about. Maybe she had a particularly good Friday night that was going to last through today…" Clairy mused.

"Then I don't know who this could be," Mim said with a shrug.

Both Clairy and Mim went to the front door. Clairy opened it, and standing just outside the screen door on the covered front porch was a military man—something easy to determine even from a cursory glance because of the camo pants tucked into combat boots, a khaki-green crewneck T-shirt and the ramrod-straight stance.

Before Clairy had gotten beyond the clothes and posture to look at the face, Mim said, "Quinn!"

Quinn Camden?

Oh, great…just my luck…

Quinn Camden had sucked up every minute her father had had from the General's first visit to Clairy after shipping her to Merritt to be raised by her grandparents. And he'd gone on sucking up every minute on every other visit from then on, trailing her father like a shadow.

Quinn Camden was the person her father had thought of as the son he'd never had. The son the General had *wished* he'd had.

Quinn Camden was the man Clairy continued to have more contempt for than anyone she knew, including her ex-husband. She held him at least partially responsible for her bad relationship with her father—more so than the long absences required by the US

Marine Corps because Quinn had made himself a brick-wall barrier between her and the General in his pursuit of her father as his mentor. And nothing—not even begging him to stay away—had raised so much as a drop of compassion or consideration in him.

Tough luck.

That had been his smug reply to her plea and it still rang in her ears all these years later…

"Oh, I wish I had more time!" Mim's voice interrupted Clairy's thoughts. "I'll have to leave for a wedding any minute. But please come in! I'm so glad you could get here!"

Clairy stepped aside, unwilling to participate in the welcome.

"Clairy, it's Quinn," her grandmother said, likely realizing that the two had not seen each other since Quinn Camden left for Annapolis sixteen years ago, when Clairy was sixteen.

"Ahh," Clairy acknowledged—and not in a friendly way. She hadn't recognized him, even when she had had a glimpse of his face.

But Mim was so happy to see Quinn, and so eager to get him inside, that her grandmother didn't seem to notice that Clairy had turned to ice. And since Quinn Camden's focus was on the effusive older woman, he didn't seem to have noticed, either.

As he came into the house and Mim ushered him into the living room, Clairy remained near the front door, merely watching.

So this is you now... she thought scornfully, taking a closer look at the man he'd grown into as he and her grandmother exchanged pleasantries.

Sixteen years ago he'd been a skinny teenager with bad skin. It was no wonder she hadn't connected the man before her with that image, because as much as she didn't want to admit it, now he was a very, very long way from it.

He was at least six foot four, and the T-shirt he had on was filled out with broad shoulders, undeniably impressive muscles in a wide chest and biceps that were cut and carved.

His waist was trim, his hips were narrow, and the thighs in those camo pants looked strong enough to kick down a wall.

And when her gaze finally rose up the full length of him to take in the face she hadn't yet studied in any detail, it shook her slightly to discover that he was the best-looking man she'd ever seen in person.

In fact, he was so good-looking that she didn't know how *that* hadn't drawn her attention from the start. It was certainly a face any woman would stare at—high cheekbones, a razor-sharp, granite jaw, a straight, slightly pointed nose and an unmarred, squarish forehead. He was so supremely handsome it was difficult even for Clairy not to be awestruck.

He had dark, almost black, hair, cut short but still longer than her father's. In fact, the stubble that covered Quinn Camden's face and surrounded his solemnly sensual mouth was longer than the hair on the General's head had ever been.

As were the full eyebrows over those eyes that should have been a dead giveaway as to who he was the minute she'd opened the door—the Camden eyes that were a distinct, unique, bright cobalt blue.

They were eyes that Clairy remembered all too well looking at her as if she was an ugly bug he shouldn't have to be bothered with.

The sound of a car horn honking drew Clairy out of her scrutiny of the person she'd always considered her enemy.

"That must be Harry?" her grandmother said, making it a question she aimed at Clairy.

"It is," Clairy confirmed after a quick glance through the screen door and a wave to the former town doctor.

With that confirmation, Mim said to Quinn Camden, "I'll have to leave Clairy to tell you about the will, the library, the foundation…well, everything." Then the older woman turned back to Clairy and said, "Will you do that, honey?"

Clairy recoiled. "Me?" she blurted out in unveiled repugnance.

"Please," Mim said, making the single word more an edict than a request.

And what could Clairy say? That since she was six years old she'd wished this guy off the planet? That now, when the wound from her lack of any meaningful relationship with her father was reopened by his death, the last thing she needed was to have anything to do with the biggest cause of that poor relationship? That that was asking too much? That Mim should have an inkling of that and help her stay away from Quinn Camden, not shove him in her face?

No, she couldn't say any of that.

Instead, she said a chilly "I guess…"

At which point Mim clasped one of Quinn Camden's boulder-like biceps and said, "I'm sorry to have to run, but we'll talk soon. Mac would be so thrilled that you answered the call…"

Then the older woman rushed out of the living room, pausing only a split second to kiss Clairy's cheek. She whispered, "I know, I know, but please be good—it's what your father wanted," then went out the front door and left Clairy alone with Quinn Camden. And the full bucket of loathing that Clairy had for him.

Loathing and a sudden awareness of how she looked…

No makeup, her hair all askew, ragbag clothes.

Not the way she wanted to be seen by anyone, let alone by someone who had always had the advantage over her.

It was Quinn Camden who broke the silence then. "Clairy… I figured as much from the red hair."

Or from her grandmother calling her by name—which Clairy thought was more likely, because she didn't believe there was anything about her that would have spurred recognition in him when, all those years growing up, she'd been invisible to this guy. How unlikely was it that he had any recollection of her one way or another?

Oh, how she'd been hoping her grandmother would deal with him so she didn't have to!

But here he was, dumped in her lap...

For now, anyway.

Just do this and then Mim can deal with him from here on, she told herself.

So, reluctantly, she left the entryway to join him in the living room.

Still keeping her distance, she stayed standing and didn't invite him to sit down, either.

But just as she was about to get to the point, Quinn Camden said, "I'm sorry for your loss."

The obligatory condolences. Coming from him, it made Clairy bristle. "I imagine it's your loss, too, isn't it?" she said with an edge to her voice. "Everyone knows he thought of you as his son. And since you spent more time with him than I ever did—"

"Let's say it's a loss to us both," Quinn interjected.

She just wanted this guy out of her house!

And the only way to do that was to get on with her assignment from her grandmother.

So, not worrying if she was being rude, she said, "Mim didn't say whether or not she told you about my father's will." She didn't give him the opportunity to respond; she just launched into it. "I didn't know this, but a few years ago he bought the building that Merritt's original library was in. He bought it so that after his death it could be turned into the Robert McKinnon Military Memorial Library and Foundation. He left all of his money and tangible assets to that, and asked that I move back to Merritt to set it up, oversee the library and memorial, and run the foundation that he wants to aid veterans and their families."

She paused but, again, not long enough for Quinn to speak.

"The will also asks that with whatever time from your duties you can spare, you help with the inception of the library and memorial that will—first and foremost—honor him, his military career and legacy. His wishes were for you to make sure he's portrayed the way he would want to be portrayed. He also wanted you and your military service to be highlighted, and to have your family's service well represented, too. Once that's done, the rest of the library will be for Montana veterans past, present and future who would like to be a part of it—that will fall back into my job description because he didn't expect you to be taken away from your own service long enough to keep up with that," she explained, hearing the formality in what she'd said, the lack of warmth, the aloofness. And not caring that that was the way she'd said it.

For a moment, Quinn still didn't respond. He just

stood in the center of the living room that was in transitional disarray, his arms crossed over his middle, his handsome face somber.

Then, with a note in his deep voice that made it seem as if he wasn't sure he should say it, he said, "I know. Mac told me when he bought the old library building and what he wanted done with it, what he wanted you to do, what he wanted me to do. We've talked about it since then. He gave me things of his that he wants put on display. He told me what he has stored in the attic here so I'd know to look for more of it... What to look for..."

"Of course he did," Clairy muttered dryly.

How stupid was she to have believed her father would have left his valued protégé in the dark just because she hadn't known a single thing about any of this until she'd read the will? And when would she learn?

"I'm sorry..." Quinn muttered.

"For what? That you were his pride and joy? That's what you worked for, wasn't it?"

Clairy regretted the outburst the minute she let it loose.

And she had no idea why it didn't raise the satisfied smirk from Quinn that it would have raised years ago. Or—even more—why it softened his expression instead.

"I wouldn't say I was working to be his *pride and*

joy. And for your sake…for starters, it *is* one of the things I'm sorry happened," he said quietly.

Oh, sure, and she believed that as much as she believed she didn't look a mess at that moment.

Quinn Camden did seem to have mastered the art of appearing sincere, though. She'd give him that. Which she considered actually more dangerous than how he'd been as a kid, when he'd been too cocky to conceal anything. Now she had to wonder what he was covering up, because sincerity from him had to be camouflage for something.

"Anyway," she said, skipping past what she considered nothing more than a forced apology, "obviously Mim is happy that you're honoring my father's wishes, and the two of you can go on from here."

"Meaning you don't want anything to do with me."

It was a statement of fact that Clairy saw no reason to deny because it was the truth.

"I figured I'd left some bad blood with you," he said. "But maybe not how deep it goes."

She just stared at him.

"It goes pretty deep, doesn't it?" he observed.

Clairy didn't disabuse him of that notion, either.

He nodded slowly. "Okay," he said, seeming to accept the situation.

But why shouldn't he just accept it? How she felt, how his role in her father's life had affected her, didn't matter to him—and never had. Why should it have, when his goals were being accomplished?

So what if it had been at her expense? So what if his tramping over her had left marks?

"For what it's worth," he continued, "I've taken stock of some things recently and… Well, the way things were with you and your dad and me, that's been one of them."

Sure it has, Clairy thought.

"And I'm genuinely *sorry*," he reiterated, emphasizing the word that had already been bandied about a lot.

As if her lack of belief in him and in anything he was saying showed on her face, he said, "You haven't done anything you regret?"

Opening the door just now to you.

But she didn't say that. She said, "You expect me to believe that you regret what you did—willfully— for *years*? When you got exactly what you wanted? Now, all of a sudden, you're *sorry*? Please," she said facetiously.

He nodded again. "I probably have that coming…"

No probably *about it…*

He took a breath, a deep enough one to expand his already expansive chest, and exhaled. Clairy had no idea what that meant. And didn't care any more than she'd cared about omitting niceties or being polite.

But after the breath he'd drawn, he left the subject of his regrets behind and said, "Have you talked to your grandmother about how this is going to work?"

Like his previous knowledge of the will and her

father's wishes, that sounded as if he knew more than she did again.

"Mim knows how I feel," Clairy said simply.

"Maybe. But she told me I'd be working with you because this is all your baby. And I know that's how Mac wanted it—not that we work together, but that the whole project be done by you, the way you see fit. He was impressed by other work like this that you've done, and he wanted you to do something on par with that for him."

"There was nothing I ever did that impressed my father. He just didn't like that I didn't come home to Merritt after college to look after Mim. This was his way of trying to control that—it just happened to come at a time when I'd decided moving home was what *I* wanted. So you can stop trying to grease whatever wheels you're trying to grease," she accused.

Quinn Camden's bushy eyebrows arched somewhat helplessly. "I'm not trying to grease any wheels, and Mac really did admire the things you've done for vets and veterans' organizations."

"Sure," she said flippantly, clear disbelief in her tone.

"Anyway," he said, taking a turn at moving this along, "I think your grandmother isn't planning to be involved in this. I think she's counting on you and me working together."

"Well, she might have to stop counting on that," Clairy informed him.

He nodded once more. "I guess I'll leave that for the two of you to sort out."

"Do that," she said stubbornly, and with a certainty that she would not be dealing with him from now on.

"Just let me know," he said.

"Mim will."

Another nod from him. "Okay, then."

Clairy didn't verbally ask him to leave, but she did clear the way to the front door.

He got the hint and went to the entryway.

But with one hand on the screen door to push it open, he turned back to her and said, "Honest to God—"

Clairy cut him off with a glare and a raise of her chin that dared him to go any further.

He took one more deep breath, gave her one more nod that acknowledged his acceptance that there was nothing he could say to soften her and finally walked out.

Unfortunately, Clairy was left with the image of broad shoulders that V'd down to a truly great male derriere.

But none of that mattered to her.

Because regardless of what a spectacular specimen of male flesh he might be, she still resented the guy with every ounce of her being.

Chapter Two

"Were you thinking you were feeding a whole battalion today, Pops?" Quinn asked his grandfather when Ben Camden called him, his older brother, Micah, and Tanner—one of the other triplets—to the table for Sunday brunch.

"How much you want to bet the three of you are all it'll take to clear this out?" the seventy-eight-year-old challenged.

The brothers laughed, but not one of them took the bet, despite the fact that the large dining-room table was laden with serving platters of cheesy, red-and-green-peppered scrambled eggs, pancakes, bacon, Ben's homemade sausages and biscuits beside a bowl of gravy.

"And how come we're in the dining room instead of the kitchen?" Micah asked.

"Wouldn't all fit on the kitchen table," the elderly man answered simply as they each took a seat and began to load their plates.

"I thought maybe Quinn rated better than the rest of us," Tanner joked.

"It *has* been too long since he's been home," Ben complained.

And if I'd come home five months ago instead of going to Camp Lejeune to visit Mac, Mac would probably still be alive...

The thought went through Quinn's mind, bringing with it a wave of the guilt he'd become too familiar with over the last five months. And since he didn't want to get into any of it, he decided to put some effort into a lighter topic.

"So where are the newest family members?" he asked his brothers. "You're *both* engaged? And, Tanner, you resigned your commission and you have a *kid*?"

"Micah's engaged, I'm engaged—yes, I resigned from the marines, and yes, I do have a kid," Tanner said, confirming everything at once.

But Quinn wanted more out of his diversion than that, so he said, "Micah, you finally won over Lexie Parker?"

"The love of my life," Micah said without embarrassment.

"Persistence paid off?" Quinn asked.

"It wasn't persistence. I gave her years and years and years between her being my high-school crush and us meeting up again now. Then I had to work hard to clean the slate before things turned around."

"And you, Tanner—a *Markham* after all Della put you through?"

"Della passed," Ben reminded him in a hurry, as if Quinn should be treading more lightly there.

Quinn did take it down a notch, reminding himself that part of his grandfather's brief update when he'd arrived last night had included a death even more recent than the General's.

But still, he said with disbelief, "Della never gave up the ghost on you and didn't make it through giving birth to a baby that was *yours*?"

"That about sums it up," Tanner said.

"So now you're a *father* and somehow you ended up with the younger of the Markham sisters?"

"Yep."

"*And* you're resigning your commission with the marines?"

Tanner said another simple "Yep."

"You guys have been busy," Quinn said, marveling. "And where are the future wives? And...wow, I have a *niece*..."

"They had to go to a baby shower for somebody," Tanner said.

"For Shawna Schultz—we went to school with

her." Micah provided the information that Tanner was vague about.

"Wow," Quinn repeated, genuinely flabbergasted by what he'd come home to. "A lot's happened around here all of a sudden."

"You can say that again!" Ben said, as if he was slightly flabbergasted by it all, too.

But then, despite Quinn's efforts to keep this a light family reunion, his grandfather said, "I was a little peeved when you decided to go to Jacksonville—to Camp Lejeune—on your last leave instead of coming home. But now I'm glad you did. It was like fate getting you there to see Mac before it was too late."

"Were you with him when he had the heart attack?" Tanner asked.

As reluctant to talk about the death of Mac McKinnon as Quinn was, he knew it was too big an event to avoid, even if he tried to pull off another diversion.

"I left him about midnight," he answered Tanner, sticking purely with the facts. "They thought the heart attack hit about three a.m.—so, no, I wasn't with him at the exact time. No one was, or help might have been called in."

"Hard for you to lose him," Ben said compassionately. As always, he was the heart and soul of the family. "You loved him like a father."

A father who probably wanted to disown me when I left him that night.

"Mac was good to me from the minute I showed up on his doorstep when I was eight," Quinn acknowledged, the truth in that making that final evening with his mentor and friend weigh on him all the more.

"Was he sick? Were there any signs?" Ben asked.

"He was as feisty as ever. Had his usual two Scotches to end his day…" *And then maybe I ended his life…* "If he was feeling anything coming on, he didn't say it or show it."

Instead, what the sixty-two-year-old Robert "Mac" McKinnon had shown was plenty of temper to rage back at the ultimatum Quinn had given him over the mistreatment of women marines that Quinn discovered in Mac's training orders.

"When your time comes, your time comes," Tanner said philosophically.

"Worse ways to go than a heart attack," Micah added.

Quinn didn't say anything, mentally reliving for the hundredth time that last monumental argument he'd had with the General. He felt disloyal—terribly disloyal to a man he owed everything to—for starting an argument that seemed to have caused the attack and made him responsible for Mac's death. Even though it was a decision that had to be made.

He took a slow drink of his steaming black coffee, kept his hand around the cup and put his focus there to anchor himself.

Maybe he could get this off his chest.

Maybe he could talk to Ben, to Tanner, to Micah, about what he'd found out, about the fight.

This was his *family*, after all. He knew none of them would judge him.

But it was still so ugly. It had brought up so much he was still trying to figure out about how Mac might have influenced him. He didn't want to get into it over this nice meal, though. Not when it was just good to be home and with his family.

So Quinn kept his mouth shut.

"And you couldn't get any more leave time for the funeral?" Ben asked.

Quinn yanked himself out of his reverie, answering a little belatedly. "No, I couldn't. I'd used it all for that visit, and since Mac wasn't technically a relative, I would have had to pull strings to get more—"

"If anyone would have understood not doing that, it was Mac—the marine of all marines, strictly by-the-book," Micah assured him.

"Mac didn't even make it back for his own father's funeral," Ben said to support that. "He was deployed at the time, and when he finally did show up, he took some flak for not getting here. And in true Mac fashion, he said his father was already dead when he heard, so there was nothing he could do for the old man, and his duty was not to leave his command."

"Service, duty—they always did come first with him," Tanner said with more admiration than Ben's voice had held.

"That was what he was all about," Quinn said, agreeing with his two former-marine brothers. "Mac was a stubborn, tough-as-nails, old-school marine. I still can't believe he's gone."

"It's gotta be tough on you, losing someone as important as he was to you," Micah commiserated.

"Takes a while to sink in, a while more to grieve the loss," Ben added. "You still have to eat, though..."

Quinn dipped a biscuit in the gravy on his plate and pondered another diversion, so his family would see only grief and miss the guilt that came with it.

"So...am I understanding that you're here now because of Mac's will and that memorial-library thing he's having his daughter set up?" Ben said then.

Quinn nodded while he ate the bite of biscuit, then said, "I am. Mac wanted somewhere where everyone from Montana who served could be acknowledged. He asked that we make the first of the contributions from our family—Dad, us—to get the ball rolling. I know there's stuff of Dad's in the basement, Pops—if you'd dig that out and maybe go through it, see what you might want to give. And, Micah, Tanner, you guys can think about anything you have."

Quinn paused to let his words sink in, then continued with his answer to his grandfather's question. "When it comes to Mac and what I'm supposed to do, he wanted the recognition he earned—I've heard all his stories and all the stories *about* him, I've been in some of his units, been on some of his missions. I know what he was most proud of, so he wanted me to make sure it gets out there."

Maybe not *all* of it, though...

"He trusted me to get him seen the way he wanted to be seen," Quinn concluded gruffly, thinking that it was a job he would have had more heart—and stomach—for before his trip to MARSOC training camp in North Carolina, where marines became part of the elite Marine Raider Regiment.

"He wanted you in charge of that? Not his own daughter?" Tanner asked, as if it puzzled him, having no idea how touchy that issue really was.

"Yeah," Quinn answered brusquely.

"But it's his daughter who's going to run the thing," Micah contributed.

"Looks like it. Mac just figured getting his military accomplishments in the limelight was a better job for me," Quinn explained, suffering yet another twinge of guilt. "His daughter has worked for the military as a civilian. I'm not clear on the details, but she's done some things with counseling vets and fundraising for them and I don't know what all. But it's the kind of thing Mac also wanted done with this project, so he thought she could do him justice with everything else and do good for vets and their families, too. But he figured I had a better knowledge of him and his service."

"So, again, Mac thought you knew him better than his own daughter does?"

"I think he was probably right," Quinn acknowledged in an undertone that lacked the pride he would have felt once upon a time.

"But you would have to work with her, wouldn't you?" This from Tanner with some cynicism.

"I'm not sure," Quinn responded. "Mim said yes, Clairy said no way."

Tanner nodded. "That makes sense. She *really* didn't like you or how much you hung around with the General."

Being forced to recall that fact didn't thrill Quinn. "No, she didn't," he admitted.

"And you were *rough* on her."

Leave it to a brother to point that out.

"I was," Quinn agreed.

"So no surprise that she doesn't want to partner up with you on this now. What if you have to?" Tanner asked.

Quinn shrugged. "I'll do whatever I need to do for Mac's sake." But if it was Clairy he ended up working with, he didn't think it was going to be pleasant—not after what he'd seen from her yesterday. It was obviously she still had some hard feelings toward him. In fact, he'd guess that she hated his guts.

And looking at it with the clarity of hindsight, he couldn't really blame her.

Everything he'd done to get Mac to take him under his wing would have made Raina Camden proud. But now, between having come to recognize some of the flaws in the way his mother had raised her sons, and viewing the situation with Mac through the eyes of Clairy McKinnon, *Quinn* wasn't proud of it.

He'd wronged Mac's daughter in pursuit of Mac, belittling her not unlike the way Mac had belittled women.

"When will you know who you'll be working with?" Tanner asked.

"Well," Quinn answered hesitantly, "maybe this afternoon. Mim wants me at her house, which I guess is Clairy's house when Mim moves in with Doc Harry?"

"The whole town is talking about *that*," Ben said, confirming what Quinn had asked. "Two old coots getting together—some are laughing behind their backs. But I think it's great. They're both lonely, they hit it off—what's age got to do with it?"

"Not a thing," Micah assured him to smooth their grandfather's unintentionally ruffled feathers.

"Anyway," Quinn went on, "Mim and Clairy will both be at the McKinnon place today. Mim wants to meet up there later and go to the old library so I can see the space that'll be devoted to Mac. But she wasn't clear about whether it would be her or her granddaughter showing me around. As of yesterday, I left it for them to sort through, so I suppose I'll find out this afternoon if I'll be in Mim's hands or Clairy's."

Quinn was a little shaken when the idea of being in Clairy's hands shot something through him that almost seemed sexual.

How the hell could that be? Cold, angry, spiteful receptions were hardly something that turned him on.

And it wasn't as if Clairy McKinnon had bowled him over with her beauty.

Okay, maybe that wasn't exactly true…

Yes, she'd been dressed in clothes not fit to wear, but they'd still given him a glimpse of long, shapely legs and hints that there might be something luscious hidden in that sloppy sweatshirt. He had replayed that image in his mind last night before he'd fallen asleep.

And, yeah, he did have to admit that she had skin like alabaster, to go with the delicate features of her face. It was obvious she hadn't had any makeup on, but he had to admit that thinking about her last night had jarred some late-to-the-party appreciation of her beauty.

Especially when he factored in those piercing wide eyes that were bright emerald green shot through with streaks of silver.

How had he missed those years ago?

Plus, there was some allure to the elegant curve of her neck, the strength and poise in her straight shoulders, the graceful length of her slim arms coming out of those ugly, cutoff sweatshirt sleeves.

And while he hadn't been sure *what* was going on with that hair, which was the color of a shiny penny, he'd been able to tell that it was thick and wavy and lustrous.

He'd undone that messy nest in his fantasy, freeing it to fall past her shoulders, down her back…

And to top it all off, she'd also managed to smell great—a scent that was lemons and lavender and something else…

So, no, maybe at first sight he hadn't realized how beautiful she was. But hindsight had made things clear. "Earth to Quinn… Come in…"

Oh, jeez, he'd completely zoned out thinking about Clairy McKinnon!

"Sorry," he said, his attention jolted into the moment again.

"You were trying to think of a way to avoid Clairy McKinnon because you know you're in for it if you have to deal with her," Tanner mocked.

"Yeah, kind of…" Quinn said, certainly unwilling to admit what he'd actually been thinking about her. Wished he *hadn't* been thinking what he'd actually been thinking about her. And still wondering why the hell he had been!

"What were you saying?" he asked Micah.

"I said, if you don't have to be at the McKinnons' until later, you can follow me home and check out the brewery."

"And load up on some cases of beer so I can taste this swill you crapped out on the marines to make," he said, taking a brotherly jab.

"We can't all serve forever," Micah said, defending himself. "I gave over a decade and a half, and the plan was always that I'd eventually switch to brewing my *swill*. And how dumb are you to beg me to let you invest in it?" Micah retorted.

"That's right—I did, didn't I?" Quinn pretended not to remember that. "So I should have some cases coming as dividends—pay up," he demanded.

"I can use another case of the citrus dividends," Tanner said. "So I'll tag along."

"That's what you get for letting family help your start-up," Micah mock-grumbled. "I s'pose you all think I'm keeping you in beer from now on."

There was a "hell, yes," a "you got it" and an "I know I do" all at once.

Micah just laughed and conceded, "Yeah, yeah, yeah."

That launched them into a conversation about the brewery and how it was going, and Quinn was relieved to not be the center of this brunch any longer.

And if Clairy McKinnon and the image of her kept creeping into his head even as that conversation went on?

He was sure it was just because he was dreading seeing her again.

Not because he wanted to…

"You know how I feel about him! I can't believe you expect me to have anything to do with him!" Clairy said to her grandmother.

Mim and Harry had had such a good time in Billings the day before that they'd been too tired to drive home.

They'd finally returned to Merritt at three thirty Sunday afternoon and had needed to go home before coming to finish Mim's move.

By then Clairy had packed the remainder of her grandmother's things and brought the boxes onto the porch. But on the way over, Harry's truck had blown a tire and his spare was flat. So Mim had walked the last block while Harry called the local gas station to come to his rescue. Now, as afternoon turned into early evening, Clairy and her grandmother were sitting on the padded swing on the front porch with the boxes, waiting for the former doctor.

Which was when Mim had told Clairy that Clairy would need to work with Quinn Camden while he was in town.

"I *do* know how you feel about him," the older woman assured her. "I just wish you could put what happened when you were both growing up behind you." Under her breath and more to herself than to Clairy, Mim added, "I'm not even sure how much of the blame Quinn deserves."

Clairy didn't know what her grandmother could possibly think redeemed Quinn and she wasn't interested in exploring it.

Then Mim went on anyway. "I know you wanted

and expected me to be the one to work with him on your dad's memorial, but the more I thought about that, honey, the more holes I saw in it. I'd just be going through old pictures and memorabilia. I don't have any idea what you or Quinn would see as important enough to be put on display, as things that would fit into your vision of this kind of thing. I was going to tell you that you needed to be in on the Quinn part even if I was."

Clairy started to speak but her grandmother cut her off. "Then I heard from Quinn two days ago—out of the blue. *Two days ago*, Clairy. You know how it is to get leave approved in order to travel—once he got it, I couldn't very well tell him and the marines that now just wasn't good for me, could I? But it *doesn't* work for me! Not when I'm right in the middle of the move to Harry's. We've torn up Harry's house to make room, and right now we're having to search through one box or pile after another to find anything we need—it's a horrible mess that we have to get on top of! So I just have to count on you, and that's what I told Quinn—"

"I'll go to Harry's and do what needs to be done there so you can deal with that Camden jackass," Clairy declared.

"Harry would be fit to be tied if it was you putting his underwear away or deciding where his denture cup should go to make room for my denture cup," Mim balked. "Besides, not only don't I have time for anything else right now, not only wouldn't I know what I was doing, but your father also wanted *you* to do this. The library, the memorial, the foundation—the whole thing!"

"Then it also doesn't need Quinn Camden's input."

"But Quinn's input is what your father *wanted*. He wanted it so much it was in his will so he could make *sure* Quinn had a hand in it—"

"Because he thought *Quinn* was the only one who really knew him and could do him justice," Clairy retorted.

"Oh, Clairy, honey… You know I can't argue that your dad was the best dad to you—he was my son and I loved him, but I know that when it came to you, he just… He didn't know what to do with you, and instead it was Quinn who got what you should have gotten from him," Mim said, choosing her words carefully so as not to judge her son too harshly. "And since you've both grown up, it's been Quinn who had that military connection with your dad, so it only made sense to him to have Quinn be in on the memorial."

Clairy recognized what her grandmother was doing because Mim had begun doing it the day six-year-old, sad, lonely, dejected Clairy had been sent to her, and Mim hadn't stopped doing it since—Mim walked a line between wanting to console and soothe Clairy while excusing her son.

"Your dad didn't think you could have the same grasp of his work, his lifelong call to duty," Mim went on. "I couldn't, and I was a navy nurse! Your father knew that Quinn would understand the kind of thinking, the kind of derring-do, the kind of decisions your dad made along the way and what he did to earn his medals. He thought it took someone who'd also been in the trenches to know how to put him in the best light—"

"Then why not just hand everything over to Quinn Camden to do?" Clairy suggested.

"Because beyond that macho stuff, this is what you do. And your dad was green with jealousy over what you did with the Jenkins Foundation. You know how George Jenkins stuck in my Bobby's craw— the two of them competed like children, their rises through the ranks were neck and neck, and your dad was sure that George never would have kept pace with him without the Jenkins money and political connections."

Clairy was well versed in the contentions between the two men and had been surprised when the Jenkins Foundation had offered her a job. She'd been less surprised when her father had been aggravated by her acceptance of the offer, but it had been an opportunity she couldn't refuse.

"I think that was still your father's driving force in this," Mim said. "He didn't want his own career overshadowed in any way by George Jenkins, and he thought what you did with the Jenkins Foundation might make that happen. That was when he decided he wanted his own memorial and foundation, and he wanted to be sure that it rivaled George's. Until the Jenkins Foundation hired you, they weren't accomplishing much, but you turned it into a feather in George Jenkins's cap, and your dad wanted to make sure you did that same thing and more in his name. Quinn couldn't do what you'll do—your dad knew that."

And if someone else had been responsible for building up the Jenkins Foundation, it would have been assigned to them instead of me, Clairy thought, believing that—like with everything when it came to her father—sentiment or the fact that she was his daughter held no rank.

But she didn't say that. She merely said a flat, definitive "I'm not going to work with Quinn Camden."

Mim laughed. "That sounded so much like my Bobby that he could be sitting right here with us…"

"And you know that if he'd have felt as strongly about something as I feel about this, it would never have happened."

"You're right—it wouldn't have. But you're a more reasonable person than he was."

"Not reasonable enough to have anything to do with Quinn Camden under any circumstances, for any reason."

"Except if your grandma needs you to! And, Clairy, I need you to!" Mim insisted with enough forcefulness to override Clairy's refusal.

"Mim—"

"Honey, I just can't do it! So you have to!"

Clairy knew that tone, and she didn't have any recourse. She closed her eyes and shook her head in frustration.

But for her grandmother's sake, for the sake of her father's library and memory, as well as for the sake of the foundation she would now be able to spearhead—something she was excited to do—she supposed she would have to suffer Quinn and his presence.

The only comfort for her was in knowing that it would only be for a little while. Just like with her father, there was only a short window of time before Quinn Camden would return to duty.

"Oh, look, everybody's here at once," Mim said then.

Everybody? Who is coming besides Harry?

Clairy opened her eyes to find both Dr. Harry, in his old beat-up truck, and Quinn, in a much newer white truck, pulling up to the curb in front of the house.

"And why is that jackass here, too?" she asked dourly.

"I was getting to that. I'm sure Quinn won't have a long leave for this, so we shouldn't waste any of the time he has, and he'll need to know how much space you're allotting to your dad's memorial in order to decide what to include and what might have to be left out, won't he? So I thought that you could take

Quinn over to the library, give him the tour and show him what he has to work with."

"Mim…" Clairy said between clenched teeth.

"The faster it all gets done, the faster he'll be out of your hair," her grandmother explained, as if she'd read Clairy's earlier thoughts.

The older woman got up from the porch swing and headed for the steps to enthusiastically greet the new arrivals.

As she had the day before, Clairy was in no hurry to go anywhere near her old foe, so after a wave in the general direction of the new arrivals—aimed primarily at Harry—she went to the waiting stacks of boxes.

Since her grandmother was forcing her into the position of dealing with Quinn again, it at least helped that today she'd paid more attention to her appearance, so she wasn't as self-conscious as she'd been on Saturday. Her hair and makeup were done, and she had on a pair of white clam diggers with a simple, pastel green funnel-neck T-shirt.

Feeling far more confident than she had the day before, she picked up one of the boxes and carried it off the porch, heading for Dr. Harry's truck, where Quinn was helping the older man lower the rusty tailgate, and she noted that he again had on camo pants and a T-shirt. The shadow of stubble on his ir-ritatingly too-handsome face made him look rugged and so masculine that that masculinity was almost palpable, even in the open air.

As she neared the truck, Quinn met her and took the box before she could object, freeing the way for the elderly doctor to step between them and enfold her in a warm hug.

"Clairy! Welcome home!"

"Good to be home," she assured the doctor, whose white hair was still thick enough for a pompadour wave that added an inch to his height.

Still held in the hug, her eyes met Quinn's over the doctor's shoulder, and she was struck by their color all over again. But the moment it occurred to her, she looked elsewhere.

When Harry released her, he said, "Quinn has offered to help load me up, so why don't you and Mim just clear the way and let us work?"

"I didn't pack any of the boxes too heavy and I carried them all out here, so there's no reason I can't help," Clairy insisted, actually wishing the frail older man would sit on the sidelines.

"How about everyone sit it out and let me do it?" Quinn suggested.

"Oh, Harry will never do that," Mim said. "He thinks he's still a he-man."

Clairy saw Quinn fight a twitch of a smile at that, and she knew he was thinking the same thing she was—that there had never been a time when the diminutive doctor had been anything close to a he-man.

While Quinn, on the other hand…

Clairy stopped that thought the moment it popped into her head. Stunning blue eyes and he-man muscles didn't make him any less the Quinn Camden she despised.

"Let's get to it!" Harry said then, heading for the porch under the accompaniment of her grandmother's warning for him not to overdo it.

Having Quinn's help did make quick work of the chore—which was good, because Clairy had a very difficult time keeping her gaze off Quinn. Unfortunately, having the job done that much faster left her saying goodbye to her grandmother and the doctor, and now alone with Quinn, that much sooner.

"So those two are taking the leap to live together," he said as they watched the old truck go slowly down the street.

"They are," Clairy answered, unable to tell by his tone if he was for or against it.

"How old are they?"

"Mim turned eighty on her last birthday. Dr. Harry is seventy-eight."

"Your grandmother is a cougar?"

It was a joke. But was he making light of it, or making fun of her grandmother and the doctor?

"She's healthy and happy with Harry. They both figure that since they enjoy each other's company and they're good companions, they might as well spend whatever time they have left together."

"But they aren't getting married?"

"He asked and he'd like to—"

"But she wants to keep her options open?"

"She just doesn't see the point, so she's not doing it," Clairy said, still wondering if Quinn's questions were indications of the same disapproval her father had shown when Mim had announced to him that she was thinking about the living arrangement.

"She doesn't need marriage," Clairy went on, "but she's also not ready to be put out to pasture the way my father thought she should be. I'm proud of her for not letting her age hold her back." There was challenge in Clairy's voice, daring him to say anything against the elderly couple.

But rather than any kind of scorn surfacing, Quinn said, "Hey, I think it's great that neither one of them is throwing in the towel just because they have some years on them. Good for Mim. And for old Doc Harry."

Okay, so in this he didn't hold the same opinion that her father had. Clairy doubted that there were too many more ways they weren't on the same track.

Then the marine faced Clairy and said, "So since Mim just took off, I'm guessing you lost the battle over working with me?"

"I certainly didn't win it," Clairy said flatly.

"I'll try to make it painless," he offered.

It was on the tip of her tongue to say *just make it fast and get out of my sight*.

But his tone was amiable and she decided that injecting too much venom into the situation was only likely to impede their progress, so she merely nodded.

And tried not to feel the hint of engaging appeal his comment had had.

"Mim said she got you over here tonight to check out the library and see what kind of space we're devoting to Mac so you'll have an idea of how much material there'll be room for," she said matter-of-factly.

"Seems like a good place to start."

"Let me close my front door and we can walk over through the town square. Or you can drive and I'll meet you, if you want to go home from there."

"I'm up for the walk."

Clairy thought she could feel his eyes on her as she returned to the house, but she couldn't be sure until she pulled the front door shut.

She hadn't been wrong, and despite being caught at it, he didn't stop watching her as she retraced her steps to the curb. But she wasn't going to let being studied like a new recruit shake her. She could take whatever scrutiny he wanted to dish out.

As they crossed the street and headed through the square, the centerpiece of it became more and more visible—the huge bronze statue of her father that had been erected two years earlier. Merritt considered it an honor to be the birthplace of a decorated national hero and had wanted that recognized.

"I heard when they put that statue up the town council discussed renaming Merritt," Quinn said as they neared it. "Two more votes and this would have become McKinnon."

"The town likes claiming him as their own," Clairy confirmed.

She expected Quinn to say it was because her father had been a great man—or something along that line—but for a moment he was strangely silent.

Into that silence, Clairy said, "How long is your leave?"

"I took ten days."

Clairy bristled internally at the idea of spending that long a time with him and let silence reign again.

Then he said, "So do I have this right—there will be a section of the old library that will be solely devoted to Mac's life and service, a second section that will be given over to other vets and a third division that will be for serving veterans?"

"And their families," Clairy added. "The memorial and the library will be on the ground floor and will also offer a small area for enlistment brochures and materials—"

"For recruitment?"

"My father mentioned it specifically in the will— he wanted the glory of the military to inspire men to join, and information right there when he hoped it happened."

"Yeah, that sounds like him."

"The foundation offices will be on the second floor and separate from the memorial and library. That's where I'll be and so will whatever staff I can afford to help organize fundraising and meet with vets and the families of vets."

"For?"

"It will be a resource center to help or access outside help for benefits, housing, loans, education. We'll have counseling for any health or mental or grieving issues, for transitioning back into civilian life. Hopefully the fundraising will give us money to use not only to keep the doors open here, but to also eventually offer financial aid ourselves—grants, scholarships, support until benefits kick in. Whatever's needed, wherever it's needed, however it's needed."

"That's pretty ambitious," Quinn said as they climbed the steps to the gray stone two-story building Mac had purchased.

When Clairy unlocked the church-like arched double doors, Quinn caught and held the one she opened, and she went in ahead of him. He followed close behind into the dusty air of an old structure that had been idle and unoccupied for years.

"There's a cleaning crew coming in," Clairy said as she waved away some of the dust that the door had stirred up. Then, focusing on the first floor, she motioned to the few pieces of furniture that were scattered around. "I want to use the bookcases and tables that were left, so I'll need to reposition them before I can measure around them for display cases and pedestals, that sort of thing. I'm hoping to do some of that tomorrow when the cleaning crew finishes, and I'll be able to give you a more exact footage of the memorial space when I do that. But for now..."

Clairy walked around, explaining her vision of things as she went. "You might want to give some thought to how you think things should be displayed so I can accommodate it—again, cases, pedestals, maybe shadow boxes and frames if there are newspaper or magazine articles. You have more grasp on what he actually wanted used to memorialize him."

Okay, she'd managed to be less hostile as she'd talked about her pet project, but that last reminder that Quinn Camden had more insight into and knowledge of her father had hit a nerve once more and her resentment echoed in her voice.

But why—when Quinn muttered, "All to the glory of Mac..."—was there something in his voice that sounded as if a nerve had been hit in him, too?

"That was his objective, wasn't it?"

Quinn didn't answer her, and that, too, was curious when she expected him to launch into accolades about how much her father deserved glory. Instead, he merely went on. "I know *what* Mac wanted out there to represent him, not the best way to *put* it out there—display cases, pedestals… Hell, I know shadowbox*ing*. I don't have any idea what a shadow *box* is. So we really are going to have to work together…"

As much as Clairy didn't want to, she had to admit that Mim had been right—this was one of her areas of expertise and she was going to have to collaborate with Quinn in a way that not even Mim would have been able to.

"I guess so," she finally conceded with a resigned sigh of acceptance.

There was nothing left of the library tour and the dust was getting increasingly more irritating to breathe, so they went outside again.

They'd had such a late start that the sun had set by the time they left the old building, and as Clairy locked the doors, Quinn said, "I'm starving. Anything around here stay open on Sunday night these days?"

"I don't really know. Over the years, Mim has mainly come to stay with me in Denver. Even being back for good now, I didn't get in until late Friday night, so it isn't as if I know anything about what's here or what goes on or when."

"What would you say to a walk down Independence to see if we can find someplace to eat? My treat."

Clairy hadn't stopped packing boxes to have lunch, so she was hungry, too. And after a long day, the idea of returning to the empty house she'd been alone in for nearly two days, and fixing something for herself to eat standing at the counter, didn't have much draw. Even if the alternative was dinner with Quinn Camden.

The best she would allow was that he was better than nothing, and she told herself it would give her the opportunity to practice tolerating him. So she shrugged without enthusiasm and said, "Okay."

Independence was Merritt's main street. It ran through the center of Merritt proper to end at the town square. But Clairy and Quinn didn't head down Independence, because when they'd crossed the rest of the square to get to it, they discovered a food truck. According to the signs posted around it, the truck had come in for the weekend, offering fish and chips.

"Smells good," Quinn said as they approached it. "Want to keep going or try this?"

Quick, easy, closer to her house than if they went the rest of the way down Independence, more informal than a restaurant...

"I'm fine with this," Clairy answered. "Nobody's using the chess tables—we can sit at one of those," she suggested with a nod to the north.

"Great."

They went to the end of a lengthy line made up of people neither of them knew, and before too long, they were sitting across from each other on the cement benches, their meals in front of them on the chess table.

As they began to eat, they talked about the growth and change in Merritt that not only brought in food trucks, but also meant that neither of them recognized anyone in the square tonight. They also appreciated the food that wasn't fancy, but that they agreed was great.

Then Quinn said, "So I don't know a lot about what you've done since I left town…"

"You didn't know anything about me when you were *in* town—except that I was in your way."

His grimace showed some remorse, but was also a concession to the fact that that was true. "I know I was a jerk to you in the old days—I told you I'm sorry for that. I wish I could make it up to you, and I'd like to find a way…"

His tone and his expression were solemn, and as if to let her know how serious he was, he laid both forearms on the table on either side of his food and looked her squarely in the eye.

"But in the meantime," he continued, "maybe we could start over? Do things differently now? We're not kids anymore, Clairy. We're connected through your dad…" He added that last part cautiously. "Would it be so bad if we got to know each other? Even a little? Maybe then I'd have a clue how to…I don't know… like I said, make up for being so lousy to you somehow."

Everything about him said that he honestly meant what he was saying, and still, Clairy's first inclination was to shoot him down, to make it clear that there wasn't anything he could do—because there wasn't.

Her father was gone, and gone with him were any thoughts, any hopes, any fantasies she'd had of somehow, somewhere down the road, reaching a point where Mac might recognize that he had a daughter, that he might even appreciate that fact, that he might acknowledge her, show her some kind of affection.

Now any chance of that was lost. Lost to all those years when Quinn *had* been close to him.

"I don't know what you're thinking, but whatever it is, I can see you getting madder and madder at me," Quinn said, injecting his voice into what was going through her head. "But, *please*, can we step onto a new path here? There are things I know now that I didn't know before. Things that make me even sorrier for the way I treated you. Things that are making me take a look at myself in a pretty harsh light… But there's no question that you are where I first went off track and I really—*really*—want to do anything I can to set that right."

That was a surprise. Mr. Tough Luck was questioning something? Doubting himself somehow?

And what *things* did he know now that he hadn't known before? What things had made him sorry and caused him to see himself in a harsh light? Were they the same things that had caused that remark about the memorial being to the glory of Mac?

Quinn certainly had her curious, if not any more likely to forgive him.

"What *things* do you know now?" she asked.

He shook his head, and his expression was so troubled, it increased her curiosity even more. "I can't talk about it yet...wheels are in motion...but..." He shook his head again. "But when it comes to you...could you just give me a little bit of a break here?"

There was such distress and uncertainty in his tone, in his furrowed brow, that it gave Clairy pause. He'd always been so obnoxiously sure of himself, of what he wanted, of how to get it. This was not the Quinn Camden she'd ever seen before. The Quinn Camden she knew. And while before she'd thought that he'd merely mastered the art of *appearing* sincere, this time she thought he actually was.

"Is it something to do with my father?" she asked.

"Just...can we please have a fresh start between the two of us?" was his only response, stubbornly sidestepping her question. "Just you and me? Can you put hating my guts on hold a little? Let me sort out what I need to sort out, and while I do, maybe if we get to know each other, try with each other, things will be better..."

More *things*...

But Clairy had to admit that he'd intrigued her.

And because of that—and in the interest of learning the secret that was niggling at him—if she had to let him feel as if he was getting to know her, if she had to put some small effort into getting to know more about him, she couldn't see any harm in it. It would all be superficial, and if it netted her some satisfaction to her curiosity, it might be worth it.

"Okay," she agreed.

Quinn seemed to relax enough to go on eating, and after a few minutes of silence, he returned to what he'd been saying before. "So college—did you stay here and commute to Northbridge for that? Or did you go somewhere else?"

"I went to the University of Colorado."

"For a degree in what?"

"Social work. I stayed there for my master's, with a special interest in military social work and counseling."

"You wanted to do something with the military but as a civilian?"

"You know my father hit the ceiling the few times I ever even mentioned joining the military—that cured me of that notion. So, yes, as a civilian. At first I was thinking more about doing something for the *families* of people in the military," she qualified. "And when I looked into different areas of social work and read that an understanding of the culture of the military was a big plus in that branch—"

"You knew you were tailor-made," he said, finishing for her.

"I definitely had experience," she said. "When I graduated, I did counseling on a military base for nearly a year."

"With just families or with vets?"

"Both. But I got more of an understanding of what good I could do with vets, so when I had the chance, I went from that to being embedded with a unit at Camp Lejeune in North Carolina."

"Embedded," he parroted, as if he had his own meaning for the word and didn't know how it applied to her work. "That means you did what?"

"I was civilian personnel doing nonmedical counseling *only* with vets there—quick fixes mainly to help build skills, keep marines who hit a relatively minor glitch functioning in the job rather than needing extended psych leave or medical discharge or retirement."

He nodded, but Clairy could tell he'd never hit one of those glitches, and she had the sense that he hadn't even been aware the service was available.

"How did you get from that to the Jenkins Foundation?" he asked.

"I...had occasion to meet General Jenkins's wife at Camp Lejeune—"

"Ahh..." Quinn mused. "The youngest Jenkins son was there. Scuttlebutt had it that he wasn't thrilled to be a marine like Dad and had a lot of issues. Were you in on that?"

Confidentiality didn't allow Clairy to speak about that, so she said only, "I just met Mrs. Jenkins there. The Jenkins Foundation wasn't really a go-to then and she was trying to get word out that help was available through them. After getting to know her, the foundation offered me the position as their liaison with military and nonmilitary agencies—"

"Did who you are have anything to do with the offer? Because Mac thought they recruited you—and you took the job—just to get his goat."

"I know. He saw it as me turning traitor, for some reason." And his anger had led to one of the rare times she'd heard from him. "But it didn't have anything to do with him. It came out of Mrs. Jenkins liking me." And appreciating the help she'd given to her son.

"Did you do counseling for the foundation or just the liaison thing?"

"They were so poorly funded at the start that I wore a lot of hats—the same way I will now to get this started. I did counseling *and* the liaison thing, fundraising, everything and anything they needed. Olivia Jenkins and I worked side by side."

"That's where you learned about shadow boxes?"

"Eventually. When General Jenkins retired, his wife wanted to retire with him, and she made me head of the foundation in her place. That's also when

General Jenkins wanted *his* library established. That's where I learned everything you'd ever want to know about shadow boxes."

Quinn laughed—it was a deep laugh that made some kind of strange ripple go through her, as if she liked that he'd appreciated her joke.

She didn't have time to analyze it before he said, "I think that counts as a meteoric rise through the ranks."

"And did my father think that was just to *get his goat*, too—me not only working for his nemesis, but also doing well with them?"

"What he didn't like was anything or anyone that did well *for* General Jenkins. And you did a lot of that. Before you went to work for them, word around was just that it was some vanity project to occupy Mrs. Jenkins. Then it started to gain some ground, which was apparently due to whatever you were doing, and there were kudos for the foundation and for General Jenkins as a result. And when that got topped off by the Jenkins Library? That put Mac over the top and it *did* get his goat, whether that was anyone's intention or not," Quinn said.

"It wasn't mine and I don't think it was anyone else's, either. Mrs. Jenkins genuinely wanted the foundation to do good work—she just didn't really know what she was doing. And she and I hit it off— the whole thing was *in spite* of who I was related to, not *because* of it." At least, that was what Clairy had believed and hoped was the case.

"Good work speaks for itself," Quinn said, as if he didn't doubt it or that she *had* done good work.

And she realized that somehow—along with liking that he'd gotten her humor—she also liked that acknowledgment.

But that didn't mean that she liked *him*. Or talking to him. It didn't mean that she was *enjoying* this—as if it was dinner with some sizzlingly hot guy who had accomplishments of his own, but who was interested in her and what she'd done in the past, who seemed impressed by it, respectful of it. What she was finding pleasure in was letting this guy who had always dismissed her know that she was no slouch.

Although she was also aware of the fact that his interest was unwavering and that it made his blue eyes seem even more blue when they were so intent on her.

They'd been talking for long enough to have finished eating, for the square to have nearly cleared out and for the food truck to have closed down. All without Clairy having been aware of anything but Quinn.

But now that she'd noticed, she began to gather the remnants of her meal to signal putting an end to the evening.

For a moment, Quinn just kept looking at her, a quizzical expression on his ruggedly handsome face.

Clairy didn't want to read too much into it, but she

had the sense that his eyes *were* opening to her as more than the mere obstacle she'd been in his quest to know her father.

Not that it mattered.

Then he cleaned up after himself, too, and once they'd deposited their trash in the nearest receptacle, they headed back in the direction they'd come.

As they passed by the old library, Clairy was searching for something to say to fill the silence that had fallen between them once more. "If you'd have driven around ahead of me, you'd be at your truck now."

"I'd have still made sure you got home," he said in a way that she would also have liked had this been a date.

He nodded toward the library and said, "Tomorrow when the cleaning crew finishes, do you have help moving those old tables and bookshelves in there?"

She didn't. "The floor is smooth and flat. I think I can slide them."

"The tables, maybe. But those bookshelves? They look pretty heavy. Can I come and help?"

With that abundance of muscle power she'd seen at work earlier loading Harry's truck?

That seemed like an offer too good to refuse.

Plus, she reasoned that the quicker that work got done, the quicker they would have a better picture of the space allotment for the memorial, and the quicker he could spend the rest of his time here with his family instead of with her.

"You *would* go away with the measurements you'll need," she said to make it seem as if it was to his advantage, too.

"So just give me a time."

"Cleaning will take most of the day. I wasn't planning to go in until three thirty or four, when they're done."

In other words, into the evening, much like tonight.

"That's fine. I don't have any pressing engagements," he joked.

And for some reason, that particular turn of phrase made her wonder about his personal status—if he might be involved with someone, if he might be engaged…

Which brought to light for her that she really didn't know much about him.

Not that that mattered, either, she told herself sternly.

Furniture moving—that's what you're talking about, she reminded herself.

"Okay, then, if you're willing, I won't turn down help," she agreed in a businesslike voice. "I'll text you when I know the cleaning is close to ending, and—"

"I'll meet you at your house, and we can walk over again," he said, as if he might have liked or enjoyed doing that tonight.

They'd reached his truck, which was parked in front of her house. Clairy stopped so he didn't go any farther with her.

"Okay, up to you," she said, agreeing to the walk, too, as if she didn't have any preference at all.

Again, in an effort to keep him from going all the way to her door, she said, "Good night," and headed up the walkway to her porch.

As she did, she was thinking about the hours that had just gone by, and she realized that if she *had* to be honest, her time with him tonight had been surprisingly not awful.

And that she didn't really mind that they wouldn't just be meeting at the library tomorrow.

That she didn't really mind that they'd have another walk together.

Chapter Three

"Engaged? Wow... Congratulations!" Clairy said to her childhood friend Marabeth Hawn.

Marabeth had made a second offer to help Clairy unpack on Monday, and when Clairy opened the front door late that morning, Marabeth had given Clairy a spontaneous hug and, rather than saying hello, said, "We're engaged!"

Now that Marabeth was in the house with the door closed behind them, flaxen-haired, freckled, girl-next-door-pretty Marabeth added, "That's why I flaked out on helping you unpack on Saturday—Brad proposed Friday night and we wanted to go to Billings to tell our parents. They're all so excited!"

"Well, sure," Clairy said, trying to hide her own

lack of wholehearted enthusiasm for the joining of her best friend and Brad Nelan.

"Remember that you said you'd be my maid of honor," Marabeth said. "Or is it *matron* of honor once you've been married, even if you're divorced?"

"I like maid of honor—I'm not sure my marriage counted for much of anything, so it doesn't get to make me a *matron*," Clairy said with some humor. "And, yes, I remember that I said I'd be your maid of honor, even if it was when we were twelve."

She stopped herself short of saying she just hoped Marabeth was making the right choice in husbands.

Clairy and Marabeth had been best friends since preschool, and that hadn't changed even when—after two years of college together in Colorado—Marabeth had decided college wasn't for her and gone home to run her parents' Laundromat so they could move to Billings.

Even though they hadn't lived in the same city since they were both twenty, they were still closer than a lot of sisters.

Having decided she could use Marabeth's help moving into the master bedroom, Clairy led the way upstairs. Once she'd explained how she wanted the closet organized, the two began to transfer clothes from wardrobe boxes into the walk-in.

"Have you set a date?" Clairy asked, still attempting to conceal her doubts.

"As soon as we can," Marabeth answered. "We're

going to get a list of earliest-available dates for the church, reception venues, the catering, all that stuff. I'm so glad you're here now so we won't have to work around when you could get away from Denver as one of those earliest-available dates. And you can help me do everything!"

Clairy bypassed the wardrobe box full of floor-length formal designer dresses she would likely never wear again, thinking that she would just leave the gowns hanging in the box and put the box in the basement. Then she opened a second cardboard wardrobe with her work clothes in it.

As she handed her friend an armload of those, she said, "Helping with everything is the maid of honor's job."

She'd intended to sound enthusiastic, but it hadn't quite made it and had alerted Marabeth. "We've been dating over a year, Clairy. Every time I see you being leery of me being with Brad, I tell you the same thing—he's not the way he was when we were kids."

When they were kids, Brad Nelan had been Quinn Camden's best friend. Brad had been with Quinn—and Quinn's brother Tanner—when Clairy had begged Quinn to stay away from her father. After Quinn's refusal, when he'd mocked, "Tough luck," Brad had joined Quinn in sneering at her, and together the two of them had ridiculed her mercilessly, humiliating her in a cafeteria full of kids. It had added to her resentment and anger at Quinn and strongly colored her opinion of Brad, too.

Even though Clairy didn't say anything to her friend's chastisement and only raised her eyebrows innocently, Marabeth went on, "I know that Brad was just as awful as Quinn Camden was when we were in school. I didn't like either one of them any more than you did. They were both full of themselves. But Brad grew out of it. You'll see when you get to know him again."

More of that getting-to-know-someone stuff.

"I know you," Clairy countered, "and you're still the same person you always were. You know me, and I am, aren't I?"

"Yes, but that doesn't mean that people *can't* be different when they grow up."

Recalling something else about that confrontation years ago, when Marabeth had been with Clairy for moral support, Clairy said, "They weren't very nice to you, either, when you told them to stop being so mean to me."

"I know—Brad called me a little bitch. We've talked about that. I guess when he did that, Tanner got on him for going too far—"

Unlike the derisive Brad, Tanner—one of Quinn's triplet brothers—had stayed silent through Quinn's response to her entreaty.

"Brad said he knew he'd gone too far," Marabeth defended her fiancé. "He apologized. He said his mouth got away from him, and if he had it to do again, he wouldn't have ever called me that. And you know we've had a few big fights—yours is the shoulder I cry on—and he doesn't fight like that anymore. He's a grown man who knows how to control his temper and his mouth. He's kinder. He's sensitive. I'm telling you, he's not that kid anymore."

For her friend's sake, Clairy hoped that was true and merely nodded.

"Go ahead, reserve judgment. You'll see," Marabeth insisted, her connection to Clairy giving her insight into Clairy's thoughts even with Clairy's attempts to conceal them.

When they were finished with the clothes that needed to be hung, they opened the boxes with shoes in them and went to work on the closet floor.

"I saw Quinn when I went in to check on the Laundromat before I came over," Marabeth said. "He was outside of the bakery with his older brother, Micah. I told you Micah and Lexie Parker both moved back to town, that he's opened a brewery and she's taking over the bakery."

"You did," Clairy confirmed.

"Anyway… Quinn… Whew! Life has been good to him in the looks department!" Marabeth said, marveling. "I'm not sure I would have known who he was if he'd been alone. No receding hairline, and what a body that guy came into!"

If there was one thing Clairy didn't need, it was

to have Quinn's looks brought to mind. Regardless of how hard she'd tried since setting eyes on him on Saturday, she just couldn't shake the ever-present mental image of him.

As if Quinn's looks weren't getting to her, Clairy said, "You can't judge a book by its cover."

"Maybe you can't judge it, but you can sure enjoy the picture before you start turning the pages," Marabeth muttered.

"I think I'd rather just keep remembering what's written on those pages."

"Unless it's changed—unless *he's* changed, the way Brad has," Marabeth said stubbornly.

Quinn *had* seemed slightly different last night, Clairy thought. But she knew telling her friend that would only encourage Marabeth. And Clairy really didn't believe that any genuine change had taken place in Quinn, nor would it have carried any weight with her.

He might be astonishingly hot, and he might have somehow evolved—although she wasn't sold on that possibility—but even if he'd grown up into the perfect man, the way Marabeth seemed to believe his friend had, it wouldn't change anything for Clairy.

To her, he was still the same kind of man her father had been, the same kind of man Jared had proved to be—someone who put everything and everyone second to himself and his career. And while the military might be an admirable career—more admirable than Jared's as a wheeler-dealer real-estate mogul—for Clairy it was a reason equal to Quinn's past bad actions to keep him at arm's length.

Certain that she was not at risk of succumbing to anything about Quinn—despite the fact that for two nights already she'd fallen asleep with thoughts and visions of him in her head—she decided to at least indulge Marabeth's belief in her new fiancé.

"The only thing that matters to me is if Brad has changed, so I'm trusting that you're right about him," she told her friend.

Then she put every effort into the right arrangement of her shoes so that maybe she could think about something—*anything*—other than Quinn Camden and how he looked.

Marabeth left at three thirty, and minutes later Clairy got word that the cleaning crew at the library was finished.

She could have texted that information to Quinn and gone on to work in the library dressed as she was—old tennis shoes, yoga pants and a nondescript T-shirt, her hair in a ponytail.

But that wasn't what she did.

Instead, she decided to shower and change clothes first.

Once in the shower she also washed her hair, and afterward, while she was bent over to blow it dry—

upside down, to add volume—she gave a lot of thought to what she was going to wear.

By the time her hair was dry, she'd decided that even if her next job of the day was furniture moving, she was still going to wear one of her best butt-hugging pairs of jeans and a plum-colored T-shirt with short sleeves gathered at her shoulders and a sweetheart neckline that displayed a hand-crocheted lace insert.

She argued with herself about wearing the sandals she wanted to wear, but that she knew were a bad choice as moving-furniture footwear, and instead chose something only somewhat less inappropriate—closed-in ballet flats.

Then she applied more-than-daytime-but-not-all-the-way-to-evening makeup before she went to stand in front of the full-length mirror on the closet door for a final inspection.

She wasn't happy with herself for having had Quinn on her mind again as she'd gotten ready, but she felt good in what she was wearing, in the way she looked. Confident. And she told herself again that confidence could only help when she was dealing with him.

Then she turned away from the mirror and texted him that the library was ready for them.

Quinn had not dressed up to move furniture, Clairy thought when he arrived half an hour later. She watched him park and get out of his truck.

He had on a khaki-green, short-sleeved crewneck T-shirt tucked into tan cargo pants that could barely contain his long legs and robust thighs. Again, a sexy scruff of beard shadowed his face, but still there was nothing that said he'd put thought into what he had on, and somehow that caused Clairy to feel slightly at a disadvantage.

Not wanting that to show, she adopted an all-business attitude, squared her shoulders, grabbed her notebook, pen and tape measure, and went out to meet him.

"Do you need to go inside for anything?" she asked.

"Nope. But hello," he said to her omission of a greeting.

"Hello," she echoed as she reached back into the house to close the door, hearing the irritation in her voice that he had no way of knowing was aimed at herself for having slightly overdone it to dress as if this was a casual first date.

As they crossed the street to get to the town square again, he nodded at her three-ring binder and said, "What's that for?"

"I was here about a month ago and made some rough sketches of the library's floor plan. I've been working on the layout of this, but I have a couple of different formations—I need to see what will work best for placement, for distribution of the displays, for flow."

"But Mac will still take front and center…"

Clairy wasn't sure whether that was to verify that nothing had changed from what she'd told him about the placement of the memorial last night, or if Quinn felt the need to protect her father's interests. That possibility irked her, so when she answered, the irritation in her voice this time *was* directed at Quinn. "It's his memorial and his money paying for it, isn't it?" Clairy said as they reached the library and she unlocked the front doors.

The inside was in much better shape than it had been the night before. There was no dust in the air or on any surface and the tile floor glistened. The wood and brass of the staircase and second-floor railing, as well as the wood-and-brass doors to the old elevator, had been polished. Every window sparkled, the walls had been washed, and the air carried the scent of cleaning solutions.

"This is a big difference," Quinn commented as he closed the doors behind them.

"Are you kidding? They did a fantastic job! Way more than I hired them to do."

"Like you said, folks around here think highly of your dad—I'd say they pulled out all the stops for him."

"I guess so," Clairy said more to herself than to Quinn, having a moment like many she'd had in her life when she felt at odds with the way her father was perceived and her own experience with him. And she wondered again, too, if the blame for her problems with him rested on her...for no reason she'd ever been able to completely determine.

Certain that if she said that to Quinn he would tell her she was definitely to blame, she didn't. She did what she'd done often—unless she'd been talking to Mim—and kept quiet.

One of the smallest of the abandoned tables was near the entrance. The tables and bookshelves had also been polished to a shine, and Clairy used the first one she came upon to set down what she'd brought with her.

Then she opened her binder, released three floor plans from the rings and spread them out separately. She explained to Quinn that she needed the exact measurements of the bookcases, the tables, the walls and floor space, and they went to work.

Although it might not have been quite as precise, she could have done the measurements on her own. But when it came time to move furniture, she quickly realized that without Quinn she wouldn't have gotten anywhere.

The tables were so heavy they would have been difficult for her to even drag, but there was no way she would have been able to budge the three bookcases.

In fact, she was awed by the fact that Quinn could. But with little more than the two of them tipping them onto his back and her guiding them as he slid them across the slick floor, that was what he did. It was a Herculean task that seemed to Clairy like asking too much of one man, but he managed it anyway.

He also shocked her by how easy he was to work with—that he didn't need to be the boss, that he took her instruction. It was one thing that was *un*like her father.

To her grandparents, Mac's visits were not the arrival of an exalted military leader—they were merely having their son home. They'd frequently asked him to do things around the house that they needed help with. Clairy had never once seen her father doing those things without Mac discrediting what they wanted done, how they wanted it done and, ultimately, either doing it the way he saw fit or hiring someone he ordered around like a mule to do it his way. And always, it was whether her grandparents liked it or not.

She'd anticipated that same behavior from Quinn and had been determined to stand her ground. But it wasn't what she got from him at all, and that was a pleasant surprise.

It was eight o'clock before they finished, and not only did Clairy end up with the work done and a slew of images of Quinn's muscles and the man himself that she knew were going to linger, but she also felt guilty because of the difficulty of the work itself and obligated enough that she thought she should at least feed him.

Which she told him when she invited him to go

home with her for the beef bourguignon she'd had slow-cooking since early that morning.

"After breaking your back, I probably owe you a massage, too," she said as they locked up the library.

Not until she saw the slow smile that erupted on his usually stoic face and the extra glint that came into his blue eyes did she realize that it sounded as if she was volunteering to do the massage herself.

"Oh, I didn't mean *I'd* give it… I meant I should probably pay for you to have one—given by some-one else."

Her own faux pas flustered her, cost her a mea-sure of dignity, and she waited for the old Quinn to make some kind of embarrassing comments that would make it worse.

But as they retraced their steps across the square, he just laughed a little and said, "I'm fine."

Clairy wished *she* was and used the walk to take deep breaths and gain some control before they reached her house.

He accepted the beer she offered him as she pre-pared the side dishes, but Quinn insisted on pitching in, unlike her father, who would have taken his beer and sat down until he was served.

It wasn't too long before her small round kitchen table and spindle-backed chairs were brought in from where the movers had left them in the living room and Clairy and Quinn were sitting down to eat.

Quinn had high praise for her burgundy stew served

with mashed potatoes, salad and French bread. That, too, was not something she'd ever heard her father do. Criticize, yes. Compliment, never.

Then Quinn said, "The place doesn't look like I remember it."

"After Grampa died, Mim made a lot of changes, upgrades. The house was originally built by my great-grandfather on Mim's side and not much had been done to it over the years, so it needed some work. Mim said while she was at it she was going to spruce it up because she was sick of living in a barracks. It was an argument she and Grampa had over and over— I guess it was his military side coming out, but he wanted everything green or brown, and he nixed anything he considered *frilly* or *flowery* or *girlie*. He and my dad ganged up on her every time she wanted to change anything, and she gave in until after Grampa passed. Then she did what she wanted—even though my father still didn't approve."

"It isn't frilly or flowery or girlie," Quinn mused as he glanced around. "Just... I don't know about that kind of thing... Brighter, I guess..."

"Since I was next in line for the house, I got to be in on her decisions, and brighter, more open, was what we both wanted. Now I don't really have to change anything—I'm just moving in. Which is nice."

"You didn't want to feel like you were living in a barracks?" he joked.

"I was never into anything military-ish."

"Is that how you rebelled?"

"Maybe," she allowed. "I know the things that my father was more interested in than me have always just not been...my favorite things."

Quinn laughed wryly before taking a slug of his beer. "Things like me," he said. "And me not being one of your favorite things is a hell of an understatement."

He still wasn't one of her favorite things, but she had to admit that she hadn't chafed too much at the time she'd spent with him lately. In fact, she might have almost verged on liking it. A little.

It was strange. And confusing. And certainly nothing he needed to know. So Clairy ate rather than respond to his remark right away.

When she did, she decided to toss the ball in his court. "If our positions were reversed, how would you have felt? What if you'd been his son, dying for his attention, and I'd come along to take it all instead, leaving you out in the cold?"

"I didn't take *all* of his attention," Quinn scoffed, as if she was exaggerating. "I mean, whenever he was in town I was here a lot, but—"

"Every waking hour."

"No," Quinn contradicted. "I was here in the mornings before you were even up, so I wasn't taking anything away from you. Zero four thirty on the dot, which is when he told me to be here for PT—"

"PT—physical training. The way marines are

trained in boot camp," Clairy said to make sure he knew that while she might not have been included, she was still well aware of that time he'd spent with her father.

"You could have joined us," he said.

"I asked to. Mac said a loud, resounding *no*, that I'd get in the way. For years—until I was a teenager and finally gave up—I got out of bed every one of those mornings hoping he'd give in and let me do it, too."

That brought a deep scowl to Quinn's face. Deeper than seemed warranted. "I didn't know you were hanging out somewhere *wanting* to be there."

"I was sitting on the top step upstairs when he came out of his room. I made him pass by me to get to you, thinking that eventually he'd give in and tell me to come, too. But it was off-limits."

"It was just a workout, a tough one, but that's all. It wasn't anything you couldn't have done…" he said, as if questioning the reasoning in her father's exclusion of her.

Clairy didn't know why the information seemed to have struck him the way it did, but she merely went on, opting to voice her grievances since she seemed to have the opportunity.

"You showed up here the first time he came to visit me—the *first* time. My mom had just died in a car accident, and the day after her funeral he packed me up and handed me over to Mim and Grampa to take home with them. For three months after that, there wasn't a phone call from him, a letter, not even a postcard—"

"He probably had a mission or something that didn't let him contact you."

"Now you sound like Mim—making excuses for him. I felt like he'd died, too," she admitted. "Then he finally came for a visit—I was already in bed for the night, and when I heard his voice, I came running out. He barely said hello to me and ordered me back to bed, said he'd see me in the morning. But in the morning—when he was still having his coffee and reading the newspaper, and I wasn't allowed to interrupt—there you were, knocking on the door, asking to see him. He barely looked out from behind his paper, but when he saw you through the screen, *standing there like a little recruit*—that's the way I heard him describe it once—he told Mim to let you in. And that's all it took for *you* to have the attention I'd been waiting for. Then and from then on," she said, her tone heating up. "He was going to make *his* kind of marine out of you—*because the service needed more of them and was getting less*, according to him."

"From my side," Quinn said calmly, "I just wanted to be in the military like my dad had been—all my brothers did. When I started to piece together that Merritt was the civilian home to someone who I'd heard grown-ups say was on his way to military greatness, a bulb went off over my head—I got this idea that maybe I could get him to take me under his wing. I'd been waiting and waiting to hear that he'd come to town, so when my grandfather said it over breakfast that morning, I went running out without even eating and hightailed it to your place."

"To announce that you wanted to be a marine just like Mac," Clairy said, derisively reiterating what Quinn had said that morning when Mim had let him in. "You couldn't have said anything he wanted to hear more. And there you were," Clairy repeated, "his own little devotee. After that, everything was a test to see if you really were or could be like him. A challenge that was right up his alley, that gave him something to do whenever he was in boring old Merritt to see boring old me... While he thought you were great."

"I just did whatever he told me to do—"

"Following him around like a shadow—"

"Not if it was during the school year—then I left here after PT and didn't come back until later," Quinn said, sticking with his claim that he hadn't taken up *all* of her father's attention.

"That didn't free up time for me to have with him—I was in school, too! And the minute I came home, you were here."

"Okay. But I was only here until dinnertime. Then I had to go home—"

"There were plenty of nights when you went on

night maneuvers or night marches or reconnaissance or night surveillance. And even when it wasn't playing war, there were also more dinners here than I can count where you went from the dining-room table to the den for him to quiz you on strategy, tell you war stories, reenact battles with his dumb toy soldiers. Or you just sat around watching war movies with him!" she spluttered.

"None of that happened until I was a lot older, until I had my driver's license and could go out at night. For all those years before that, I had to be home to eat and then stay there. It was family time—the same as it was here."

"Ha!"

"You're claiming I *didn't* have family time?" he asked, their debate at full steam although his voice was even and only Clairy was clearly angry.

"I'm telling you that I didn't have family time even after you left and *that* was your fault, too!"

"Come on," he scoffed again. "He was your *dad*... I didn't have a dad, but I was still hanging out with my mother, with my brothers, with Big Ben. Don't tell me that isn't what you were doing over here with a father you only got to be with when he was in town. Especially when you were little, long before he was running me through night training."

Quinn hadn't had a dad? What was that about? Clairy wondered. Of course he'd had a dad—his father had served in the military and was slated to go into the library…

But again, she saw this as her chance to give her side of things, and she wasn't going to veer from it to ask what Quinn meant.

"There was no such thing as *family time* with my father," she said instead, as if Quinn was delusional. "If he was here on leave, he ate dinner in the dining room and he talked to Mim and Grampa—not to me, because *children were to be seen and not heard*, according to him. At least, that's how it was with me—"

"Not much different with me, then—I was just supposed to take orders."

"But he talked *about* you—he bragged about you, about the super marine he was making out of you, about how proud he was to be doing that. Sometimes he told them something funny you'd done or said that delighted him—he didn't even talk *about* me."

"But you were here and I wasn't," Quinn insisted. "That should have counted for something."

"When it was still all about you? And how could I compete with the massive number of push-ups you'd done for him that day? Or the marsh you'd slogged through even after you'd slipped and were covered in mud? Or the funny question you asked him about latrines? How could he care about helping me with my spelling words when *you* had started to understand how to tell military time? When it was 'all hail young Quinn' everywhere I turned! One night I asked him to tuck me in and he said he was sure *you* didn't need tucking in, so why should I? Family time?" she repeated. "Once dinner was over he wanted to read or watch his TV, have his Scotch, and again, I was supposed to be *seen and not heard—that* was my family time."

"He wouldn't have known whether I needed to be tucked in or not," Quinn said, as if there was nothing else he could think to say to all that.

But it was a weak answer and he seemed to know that. He was silent for a moment, his expression showing some guilt. Then he said, "I didn't know that was how he was with you. He was your *dad*—I was jealous of that. I figured that when I wasn't around he was *being* your dad, the way I imagined a dad would be."

As if the reality was beginning to sink in, after another moment of thought, Quinn said, "But now that you say it, I do remember you trying to tag along sometimes on my days with him—training and whatever. I remember that he was a bear to you. But he was a bear to me—that was just part of it. I thought that if you wanted in, you needed to take what he dished out the way I did. Since you always went away…" He shrugged. "I figured you didn't want in, that you had other times with him."

"Other times when he wasn't turning you into his mini-marine? Other times when he wasn't devising his next test to see if you'd pass it? Other times when he wasn't busy setting up your obstacle course for the next day? He was always only here on leave—there *were* no other times!"

"Okay. Okay…" Quinn finally conceded. "You can blame me for the time I did take up. But I'm not sure there's blame for me in working so hard for him that he talked about it. And is it really my fault that he *did* talk about me when I wasn't around? My fault that he still wasn't paying attention to you?" Quinn asked in his own defense.

Clairy had that answer at the ready because it was the answer she'd clung to since early on. "Oh, believe me, my father gets plenty of blame! I never accepted Mim's excuses for him then or now, and maybe the best I could have hoped for was that he would have eventually gotten bored enough to toss me a few crumbs of attention, a little bit of acknowl-edgment. But instead, he had you to keep him from even the chance of that! He didn't go looking for you…and he wouldn't have. If you had stayed away from him *period*, then I might have been able to have the time with him that you took up. He might have gotten bored enough to *notice* me. And then maybe—even if it was just by default—we might have come to have a relationship! If you had stayed away from him, there wouldn't have been anything for him to talk about and plan for and compare me to! I might never have been able to be the son he hadn't had, but he might have come to know the daughter he *did* have!" she stressed. "Instead, he had *you* to *be* that son he wanted! And I was just left being incidental to the glory that was you!"

She'd really let Quinn have it. They'd both stopped eating, and now that he was leaning on his forearms clasping his beer bottle between both big hands and looking very serious, she waited. And wondered.

Was he really as sorry as he'd claimed to be last night? Or would he do some version of what he'd done in the past when she'd aired her resentment—would he use what she'd exposed against her? Would he goad her with it? Would there be some version of *tough luck*…

Quinn sat back and met her gaze squarely. "When it started I was just a kid, too, and no eight-year-old thinks they're doing something wrong to go after what they want—especially not if they were raised by Raina Camden. But later, when you asked me to stay away… You're right. I should have. You didn't hide how important it was to you, and it was pure selfishness on my part to ignore it."

He paused, arched his eyebrows at her and added, "I know I treated you rotten. Like I said, I was so jealous that you were Mac's kid, that you had him and I didn't have a dad at all… And…" He sighed with some heavy self-disgust, shook his head and seemed reluctant to go on, then admitted, "I thought you were just a girl…"

"So I was incidental. Not as important as you—you *are* cut from the same cloth as my father," she said snidely. "I was only incidental to him, too."

Quinn frowned at his beer again for a few minutes before his eyes returned to hers. "I can apologize again—and now, knowing even more, I *am* even sorrier and feeling like an even bigger horse's ass—"

"But all the apologies in the world can't change anything," Clairy said.

"Which is why we agreed to a new beginning last night… Did you decide there's too much water under the bridge for that?"

She'd had a full head of steam. But when she considered whether or not there was too much water under the bridge for them to move on from here, she realized that it actually had felt good to let off some of that steam. She'd finally had the chance to say her piece. And she'd said it.

Okay, maybe she'd said it loudly enough, stubbornly enough, angrily enough for him to think there was no going on from here, but the truth was that she felt as if letting off that steam had cleared the way to go on from here.

She took a deep breath, told herself to dial it back and said, "Honestly, it's good to be heard for once."

He nodded. "I'm learning more and more how important that is," he said quietly before his dark eyebrows arched up and he let out a breath that wasn't quite a laugh. "And I definitely heard you," he assured her. "I heard more things for me to know now that I didn't know before. So are we…okay? I mean, are we at least no *less* okay than we were before?"

"We're the same amount of okay," she decreed, unwilling to let him know that she might be slightly better than that.

Not that she'd forgiven him, but now that he was taking accountability for what he'd done, now that he'd genuinely listened to her side and recognized what his actions had cost her, it did help.

"All right, then…" Quinn said tentatively, as if he wasn't sure he could trust that things weren't worse between them. "I guess this is part of getting to know you? Of getting to know what makes up Clairy McKinnon?"

"That was my childhood," she said.

"And now we can keep going?" he asked.

"Think you can take more?"

"I don't know. You're tougher on me than your father ever was," he joked.

"You asked for it from him. You earned it from me," she said.

"I know I did," he admitted with a mirthless laugh. He stood to gather their dinner dishes as Clairy noted another thing that made Quinn unlike her father—an ability to acknowledge he'd done something wrong.

She stood, too, and joined in the table clearing. "You're the guest and this was repayment for your work at the library tonight—you don't have to do dishes," she informed him.

"It's late, and if we do it together, it'll be done quicker."

She didn't argue. Instead, while they worked side by side cleaning the kitchen, something new cropped up for her to wonder about. "So this is another way you aren't like my father—he did *not* do dishes—"

"*Another* way?"

Of course, he couldn't have known she'd been comparing him to Mac...

But after that slip of the tongue, she decided that the differences Quinn had exhibited might have earned him a tiny concession.

"My father wouldn't have let me—or anyone else—tell him what to do at the library tonight, and he would never have accepted that he might have done anything wrong like you just did. Now you're doing dishes. That was *not* something he would lift a finger to help with."

Quinn accepted that with a nod and made a second trip to the kitchen table for things Clairy was putting in the dishwasher.

"Where has your domestic training come from?" she asked, thinking that—especially with those looks—he was bound to have had a lot of women in his life. That there were likely women—or one special woman—in his life now.

"You can thank my mother for that—she had four

boys, so there was no sexism in the doling out of chores."

That was an answer to what she'd asked, just not the satisfaction to what she'd gone on to ponder.

"Has anyone else benefited from that training?" she inquired somewhat hesitantly, since she had no business going down this avenue and she knew it.

"I've done dishes before, sure. And laundry and vacuuming and mopping, and I can even cook a few things," he answered, apparently oblivious to what she was looking for.

"Which you've done for girlfriends? A wife?" she persisted.

"Not a wife—I've never been married. Girlfriends, sure."

Was it the thought of those girlfriends that caused his expression to tense up and some of the glimmer to leave those stellar blue eyes, or had it been brought on by her poking around in this?

Clairy couldn't be sure. But the possibility that it was caused by her poking around still didn't stop her. "Is there someone now who you should be doing dishes with?"

"No. And there hasn't been for a while… I guess for me relationships have been—"

"Incidental?" she goaded with the earlier hot-button word, guessing that—since relationships with women after her mother had not ever seemed to be more than that for her father—that was what personal relationships had been for Quinn, too.

"*Incidental* is the dirty word for the night," Quinn muttered. "But, no, my personal life hasn't been my priority. No surprise to you, I'm sure, but I've been married to the marines."

Clairy nodded as she put the finishing touches on the kitchen and reminded herself that this wasn't a subject she cared about.

Or at least it wasn't a subject she *should* care about, and yet regardless of how much she didn't want to admit it, deep down she liked that there was currently no one special in his life.

But only, she told herself, because she wouldn't have wanted him to be successfully in a relationship just as she'd failed out of one.

With the kitchen tidy again, she pivoted from facing the sink to face Quinn.

He was leaning with his hips against the counter next to her, his arms crossed over his expansive chest in a way that accentuated those biceps she'd put to good work earlier. And done no small amount of ogling in the process.

"I can't say relationships or marriage are my area of expertise," she admitted, putting an end to the subject.

He seemed to welcome that and offered a new one. "So tomorrow…exterminators are coming in to deal with raccoons in the library's rafters?"

The cleaning crew had made the raccoon discovery today and had notified Clairy about it. She'd had to take action from there and had filled in Quinn about it as they'd moved furniture.

"Right," she confirmed. "And until that gets taken care of, we're not supposed to be there."

"That works for me. I arranged with my grandfather and brothers to gather Camden military stuff. We're doing that tomorrow. How about if, once I get it all together, I bring it over here and you can go through it, see what you want, what you don't?"

"Great!" Clairy heard the overabundance of enthusiasm in that single word. Analyzing it, she realized it stemmed from having begun to think there wouldn't be a reason for them to see each other the next day, and then learning that there was…

What are you doing, Clairy?

She put effort into toning it down as she followed Quinn's lead to her front door, where he was obviously going to wrap up the evening. More neutrally, she said, "I need to get my own unpacking and furniture arranging done, so I'll do that. You can just let me know when you have everything ready for me, and we'll set a time. I'm glad we won't completely lose a day," she added, justifying her own enthusiasm.

"It might not be until later, after dinner even. Big Ben and I will get out my dad's stuff, but neither of my brothers are sure when they'll get me theirs. They just promised it would be tomorrow."

"I'll be busy, so anytime is fine, even tomorrow night," Clairy said, actually pleased with the thought of the two of them spending a quiet summer's evening sitting together looking through some of his family history.

But only because otherwise she'd just be spending a boring night on her own, not because she *wanted* to be with him.

Right?

They'd come to a stop in the entryway and Quinn had turned to face her, one hand on the doorknob.

It was absolutely, perfectly normal and aboveboard—just any old guest leaving.

But there Clairy was, with the sense that it was the end of some kind of date.

Of all things.

As she tried to squash that idea, the quiet that came between them—the fact that Quinn didn't immediately open the door and just go, the fact that he was studying her as if something about her had suddenly struck him—only contributed to that feeling.

And without invitation, Clairy's gaze went to his supple and oh-so-masculine lips, and she somehow became curious about what it was like to kiss him…

Oh, no, that can't be.

She drew herself up straighter, stiffer, and stopped *that* nonsense!

"So just let me know," she said abruptly, referring to their plan for him to alert her when he was ready to bring his family's military mementos to her on Tuesday.

He really was lost in some thought that seemed to be about her, because only her words yanked his eyes off his study of her face. "I will. And thanks for the fancy stew—it was one of the best things I've ever eaten."

Clairy remembered belatedly that she should be the one thanking him. "Oh, it was nothing compared to what you did at the library—I should have had a couple of movers..."

"Nah, no big deal. I'm here to help," he said as he finally did open the door and step onto the porch.

Clairy went out behind him, needing a hit of cooler night air suddenly—*not* because kissing was still on her mind, she insisted to herself, only because it was warm in the house.

There was no hesitation in Quinn's departure as he simply said, "G'night," and headed for his truck.

"Night," Clairy called after him, taking in a deep breath and then exhaling in a quick huff of shock at herself.

Kissing Quinn Camden? How could that possibly *ever* have crossed her mind?

Maybe it was the fumes from the cleaning solutions at the library.

Maybe they'd given her a belated buzz.

It had to be some kind of reaction to *something* other than him!

Because there was no chance it was just him, she convinced herself.

And certainly no chance that it was anything she wanted to happen…

Chapter Four

"What the hell are you doing?" Quinn asked his reflection in the mirror over the sink in his bathroom early Tuesday evening.

He had his straight razor in hand and he was about to shave the scruff he liked to grow when he was on leave.

And why was he on the verge of shaving it?

Because for the millionth time since he'd come home from the McKinnon place last night, he'd been thinking about Clairy and about the end of the evening. And about how tempted he'd been to kiss her. About how, if tonight should end the way last night did and he *did* kiss her, it might be better to lose the scruff.

"Where's your head?" he sneered at himself.

He opened the medicine cabinet and put back his razor, taking out the trimmer he used on the scruff to keep it neat. Then he closed the cabinet door more firmly than it deserved.

He'd spent the day with his grandfather, sorting through boxes of his father's things to find anything pertaining to Reese Camden's military service and hauling them upstairs to look over. Tanner and Micah had joined them later in the afternoon with their own contributions to the McKinnon library, and they'd also dug in to their father's mementos.

When they'd left, Ben had thrown two steaks on the grill while Quinn had loaded his truck with the boxes full of final choices for the library. Then he'd texted Clairy to say he could be there around seven thirty. She'd texted back that that worked for her, too, and Quinn had gone on to eat with his grandfather.

It was after that that Quinn had come upstairs to shower. And shave.

With the towel still tied around his waist, his hair damp, he'd stepped up to the sink to shave and— thinking about other things—grabbed the razor.

"You are *not* going to kiss Clairy McKinnon," he ordered his reflection, his fiercest glare enforcing the directive that no one in any unit he'd ever commanded would have dared disobey. "Not last night, not tonight, not *ever.*"

But damn, had he been close to it last night! he

thought as he turned on the trimmer and went to work with it.

He'd been close to kissing Mac's daughter...

Mac's *daughter*.

That pain-in-the-ass kid he'd always wished wasn't around. Whom he'd been jealous of. Annoyed with. And hadn't thought of beyond that.

And now he couldn't seem to *stop* thinking about her. Ever since Saturday...

Despite the fact that her hair had been wonky and she'd been dressed in clothes she couldn't possibly have thought anybody would see her in, that first glimpse of her since he'd last set eyes on her, when she was sixteen, had stayed with him. And from then on, his attraction had just escalated—in no small part because dressed in better clothes, her hair combed and wearing a little makeup made her such a knockout he couldn't keep his eyes off her when he was with her, and then he carried every detail of the way she looked home with him.

It was as if—for some reason—she'd set up residence in his head. And not just the mental image of her. There was the sound of her voice, the memory of things she said—even the hard time she gave him. Every minute they'd been together was with him continuously, regardless of how much he tried *not* to think about her. Nothing like that had ever happened to him before.

Maybe it was guilt?

That was possible, wasn't it? Especially when learning how Mac had disrespected women had left him wondering if he might have subconsciously done the same thing. He'd come to feel obliged to look back at the way he'd thought of Clairy as well as the way he'd thought of his adult relationships, the way he'd treated her. Maybe taking a closer look at her was part of that.

But that isn't all you're doing...

In fact, it wasn't even the lion's share of what he was doing.

It wasn't guilt or reevaluation of the past that had him picturing that thick, wavy red hair of hers and wondering if it would run through his fingers like silk. There was no guilt or reevaluation in fighting to keep from letting the backs of his fingers trace her cheek to find out if her skin was as soft as it looked.

It wasn't guilt or reevaluation that was going on when he lost his train of thought looking into her eyes and wondering if he'd ever seen a green so beautiful.

Or looking at those delicate lips of hers, thinking they were ripe for kissing, and wanting to do that kissing until she begged him to stop.

He wasn't remembering that she was someone he'd treated badly. He wasn't even recalling that she was someone who had a grudge against him that she was right to have. She wasn't even Mac's daughter.

She was just a delicately stunning, feisty little

spitfire who was churning up things in him at a rate no one had ever done before, with an impact no one had ever had on him...

And for no reason he could even figure out...

But she *was* Mac's daughter, he reminded himself. He didn't really know if that should make her off-limits, but it seemed as if it might. It seemed like there should be some kind of code against it.

Especially when his thoughts about her went beyond kissing. Which they tended to do as he was trying to get to sleep the last few nights...

Mac's *daughter*...

Over the years—like a father encouraging his son to find a wife—there had been any number of times when Quinn and Mac had been in a bar and Mac had jabbed him with an elbow to draw his attention to a pretty woman whom the older man thought he should chat up. There had even been a few times Mac had arranged for him to meet someone he thought Quinn might hit it off with. But never had Mac suggested Quinn take an interest in Clairy.

"Could be he didn't want you fraternizing with his daughter," Quinn told his reflection. "Could be he saw your lousy track record with women and didn't want her in line for that."

Not that Mac had ever seemed protective of Clairy.

"You probably weren't, were you?" he asked his absent mentor, his own disillusionment with Mac coming to the forefront suddenly. As did Clairy's comment last night that it had felt good to be heard...

It had taken Quinn weeks after learning Mac put women marines in jeopardy to force them out of service—or at least out of his command—to decide what to do with that information.

Mac was dead—he wasn't harassing or endangering any more women, he'd told himself. Maybe what he'd done didn't need to be known.

But then he'd also begun to analyze his own actions toward women, his relationship failures, and it was the women Mac had wronged who started to haunt him. Those women and the idea of sweeping them under the rug along with what Mac had done to them.

It had ripped him apart to realize that his loyalty to Mac, guarding Mac's reputation, couldn't be all he took into consideration. If it was, if he ignored those women and whatever damage might have been done to them and their careers, then he really wasn't any better than his mentor...

So he'd called a friend, an attorney in the Judge Advocate General's office...

His guilt over what still felt like betrayal of the man who had shaped him and his life dogged him. But since that phone call, Jill had been doing a preliminary investigation to decide how far to take what Quinn had reported. Nothing could be done to Mac posthumously—although it was Mac's reputation and the mark against him that was difficult for Quinn to feel responsible for—but one of the main things that would come out of looking into Mac's misdeeds now would be to give those women a voice. To let them be heard...

"So maybe if that happens you'll understand?" he asked the also-absent Clairy, hoping she would.

Which was something else new.

He hadn't loved the idea of telling Mac's daughter any of this, but now it ate at him to think that Clairy might turn even more against him when he did, when he had to confess that if her father's reputation was tarnished, it would be by him...

He shook his head at his reflection in the mirror. "One more reason to keep the brakes on with her," he said, thinking that it went on the list that also included his poor relationship track record and the point he'd reached since Camp Lejeune, when he'd realized he needed to reassess the way he viewed women himself and where they fit in his life, if they fit in. Or if they should be kept on a strictly R & R basis, the way his mentor had.

One thing he already knew was that, when it came to women from now on, the only ones he was going anywhere near had to be either in the military themselves—which was preferable—or be 100 percent on board with the fact that, for him, the US Marine Corps came first.

And Clairy McKinnon didn't fit either of those categories.

Add to that the fact that she was someone he'd already hurt, and he knew he shouldn't get involved with her.

"So no kissing," he reminded himself, as if saying that settled it.

Which it did—he wasn't going to kiss her.

Then, in his head, he saw her again—soft waves of red hair, alabaster skin, those green eyes.

He saw again the look that had been in those eyes at the end of last night, when all of a sudden they'd softened somehow, when a new sparkle had come into them that had been sexy as hell. When her glance had fallen to *his* mouth for a minute in what had read as a sign and had put him completely in the mood to kiss her...

"You still can't do it," he ordered his reflection.

And he wasn't going to.

So why did he reach for the beard oil that was supposed to make the stubble kissably soft?

By six o'clock Tuesday evening, Clairy had her living-room furniture arranged the way she wanted it and was ready for company.

For Quinn's company. In order for them to work tonight on his family's contributions to the library. Not for any social kind of thing.

She'd been reminding herself of that all day long.

Reminding herself that seeing him was not her preference. They were working together for a short time and that was the extent of it. She couldn't explain why seeing him kept ending with the sense that they were socializing. Socializing in a way that could end with her thinking about him kissing her. As if the socializing they were doing was dating...

But that was *not* what was going on, and as she'd worked, she'd lectured herself about it.

If it hadn't been for her father's will asking that Quinn oversee the memorial and that his family contribute to the library, she and Quinn wouldn't be having anything to do with each other.

And once his part of the job was finished, Quinn would disappear into the marines the same way he had years ago. If they ever saw each other again, it would only be by accident, when he came to Merritt to visit his family.

So by no stretch of the imagination was their being together under the current conditions *dating*, and she told herself firmly that she had to stop having any illusions about that.

It was all very clear in her head when she went to the kitchen at the end of the day. But even so, as she reheated a bowl of last night's beef bourguignon to eat standing at the counter, she went over it all again to make sure there wasn't and wouldn't be any question. There was absolutely nothing going on between her and Quinn Camden in which kissing would ever occur.

Then she hurried upstairs to the shower—again, not because she was getting ready for a date, but because she'd worked on the house all day and needed one. As well as a quick shampoo.

After that, an upside-down hair drying put waves, volume and shine into her hair before she applied evening-level makeup—only thinking of lighting and not wanting to fade into the woodwork, not considering who would be looking at her, she assured herself.

Then she chose a cream-colored crocheted top that she wore over a simple tank for modesty's sake, and a pair of denim jeans hemmed with embroidery and lace that matched the crochet pattern of the top.

Altogether it wasn't quite a sitting-around-alone-doing-nothing outfit, but it also wasn't anything she would wear for an evening out, either. So not-date-clothes for not-a-date, but still feminine and presentable.

And it was also in keeping with her goal of never feeling as if Quinn had an advantage over her again, she decided.

Which she felt like he'd sort of had when she'd drifted into wondering what it might be like to kiss him last night. An advantage she thought she'd gone on giving him when she had continued thinking about him—and kissing him—long after he'd left and right up until she'd fallen asleep.

But not tonight! Not after also reminding herself today of every problem he'd caused between her and her father, every single thing he'd ever done to cause her to dislike him.

And between forcing herself to recall his mistreatment of her and those reminders of what was really going on, as she slipped her feet into a pair of cream-colored fancy flip-flops, she felt sure that there was no chance of him getting to her tonight.

At least, she felt sure of it until she descended the stairs and, through the open front door, caught sight of him through the screen getting out of his truck.

He had on jeans and a white polo shirt, the short sleeves stretched firmly around those biceps making them impossible to ignore.

His off-duty military wear was simply serviceable attire, but the jeans and that polo shirt? They might not be dressy, but they weren't workmanlike, either. They were clothes he'd put some thought into. The kind of thought that went into socializing...

"It doesn't matter," she muttered to herself as she watched him take boxes out of the cab of his truck. "This is still strictly business—from the beginning to the end!"

Sticking with that, she went out the screen door and said, "I can take some of that stuff in."

"Hi," he said, for the second time giving the greeting she had omitted because to her it seemed too friendly.

"Hello," she responded with a touch of aloofness to once again send a there's-nothing-personal-to-this message.

She offered no other pleasantries, and merely picked up one of the boxes he'd unloaded and set on the lawn, and returned to the house.

She did hold the screen open for him once she got there, though, reasoning that it was a simple courtesy since he'd loaded himself up with the remainder of what he'd brought and his muscled arms were full.

"You got your living room set up," he observed when he went in.

"So we could work in there, maybe spread things out on the floor to get a full picture of what's here," she said, following behind him and hating herself for checking out how his rear end looked in jeans.

And judging it much, much too good...

Quinn deposited his boxes on the oval coffee table.

"I have iced tea if you're interested," she said, having already decided not to offer beer or wine in order to keep the tone not-date-like.

"Thanks," he said, his own attitude tonight seeming a bit more formal, too.

Clairy went to the kitchen and returned with two tall glasses of tea, setting them on coasters on the oak end tables that bookended the overstuffed sofa and matched the coffee table. Then she got right to the task at hand. Standing over the boxes, she said, "Let's start with the most recent stuff."

"That would be in those two small boxes." He pointed to two boxes sitting atop a larger box. "One is from Micah, the other from Tanner—"

"And from you and your other brother?"

"For now I'm only handing over a few pictures of me and your dad—they're in this file folder."

The file folder was in a second box. He took it out and handed it to her.

Clairy opened it, finding inside three photographs and a magazine article with a fourth picture included in it.

The article was on a conflict in the Middle East and the picture was a candid shot of Quinn and her father at a desert campsite. They were studying a map on a table outside an enclave of tents, both outfitted in heavy combat gear and paying heed only to what they were so seriously discussing, seemingly oblivious to being photographed.

"You're so young," Clairy observed of Quinn in the photo.

"It was the first mission Mac recruited me for," he said, his tone ringing with reverence and the flattery he'd felt at being chosen.

Clairy set aside the article and picked up one of the photographs. It was of Mac pinning a Medal of Honor on Quinn—Mac's stony expression still somehow managed to convey the pride that Clairy had never seen from him for herself. It raised envy and resentment in her that prevented her from commenting. She merely set the picture on top of the article.

The second snapshot was of Quinn and Mac in a bar, arm wrestling, the camaraderie of their relationship, their affection for each other, clear even as they competed.

That fierce-competitor facet of her father was yet another thing he'd relished having Quinn around for, another thing she couldn't participate in, and Clairy felt a second twinge of old umbrage as she saw evidence of it again.

Once more, she said nothing as she moved on to the third photograph. It was a posed picture of her father, Quinn and his three brothers, the five of them in dress blues.

"Wow, this was something," she observed, looking at Quinn in particular in his formal uniform, doing it justice to such a degree she couldn't take her eyes off him. "I didn't know there was a time when you and your brothers were all with Mac..." She pointed to Quinn and his older brother. "You and Micah..." Micah had attended her father's funeral, so she recognized him. "But I haven't seen the other two triplets since they left Merritt the same time you did. Plus, you all resemble each other so much— which is Tanner and which is Dalton?" she asked, needing to force her gaze from where it wanted to stay on Quinn's image.

Quinn told her, then explained, "That was the White House dinner honoring Mac. I'd come into DC especially for it, but Micah, Tanner and Dalton just happened to be in Washington at the same time. When Mac heard that, he pulled strings to get them on the guest list, too. We were surprised that you and Mim weren't there, but he said it was too soon after you'd lost your grandfather."

Clairy couldn't help bristling again. "I think he just didn't want us there. Grampa had been gone six months and Mac didn't even tell us about the dinner until it was over. Mim and I were both upset by that— I've never seen her so hurt and angry. But when we complained, he told us to quit *squawking* like two hens, that if Grampa would have been alive he would have asked him, but that Mim and I would have just been out of place with military men and politicians."

"God, Clairy, I'm so, so sorry..." he said, as if he'd genuinely been struck by the information.

"Did you have something to do with him not telling us?" she said suspiciously.

"No! That was lousy of him!"

Was Quinn actually admitting that? Clairy was shocked.

"Some military women and female politicians were included, too—" he said. "Of course the honoree's mother and daughter should have been asked to a White House honor presentation before me or my brothers..." He cut himself off, as if once the words were out he'd reconsidered the wisdom in saying them. Then, seeming to search for something to vindicate Mac's actions, he said, "Is it possible that he honestly did think you and Mim were still grieving?"

"I think he just didn't want us there," Clairy repeated. "I don't know if he thought we'd embarrass him in some way, or if he was ashamed of us… I don't know," she said with an echo of anger.

"I think it was just Mac being Mac," Quinn said almost under his breath but with an edge of disgust she wouldn't have thought ever to hear from him in regards to her father.

But that didn't seem possible and she decided she had to be misinterpreting something.

Then he said, "I didn't know he hadn't even invited you. I believed what he told me…"

There was definitely disgust in Quinn's tone this time, but she couldn't tell if it was disgust for Mac or self-disgust.

Quinn started to say something but stopped himself, seemed to change course, and as if falling again into his loyalty to her father, he said, "It *was* all military and political talk…"

"Excuses, excuses, excuses," Clairy muttered, wondering how many slights and old wounds would be reopened for her before this project was accomplished and she could move on to what she wanted to do—her own work through the foundation.

"But I'm sure my father would want all of those

pictures included, so thanks," she said somewhat be-grudgingly, replacing the article and pictures in the file and setting it aside.

Unable to keep some additional stiltedness out of her voice, she backtracked. "So that's all you want to contribute now?"

"Dalton and I agree that this seems like what you do when you've resigned or retired, when the last chapter has been written," he explained, as if he was glad to move on. "Micah and Tanner sent medals and ribbons they were awarded, decorations, some photographs—mainly pictures of them with buddies they want remembered—but they're both out of the service now... Well, Micah is—Tanner's paperwork is filed and he's burning off leave time, but essentially he's done, too. Dalton and I are ongoing, so it isn't time to tell those stories."

"And your brother Dalton is—obviously from the picture—a marine, too."

"He is. There *are* a couple of things he's sent to Big Ben that he said could start the ball rolling on him—they're in here, under Tanner's and Micah's things. It's a place to start on him...or maybe a place-holder for him. But other than that—"

"It isn't time to tell his story," Clairy repeated, thinking that Quinn was talking more than usual to fill the awkwardness left by the reminder of the White House dinner.

"In the Jenkins library," she went on, "there were

a few families like yours—past and present service members. The present ones were just noted as currently serving in whatever branch. We left space to be filled later." And Clairy was also eager to move on, so she opened Micah's box, then Tanner's, deciding everything they'd sent could be used. She set aside those boxes with the file folder before motioning to the rest of the boxes.

"So all of this is your dad's?"

"It is," Quinn confirmed.

"Then we can do a bigger display of his things."

"Sounds good." Quinn seemed relieved to be talking about his father rather than hers, and the change in topic also helped Clairy emerge from some of her own resurrected negative feelings.

Part of what she loved about this job was learning the unique stories of each veteran and that was what came to the surface as they began to tackle the boxes of Reese Camden's memorabilia. Her first surprise with Quinn's father was that he was in the US Air Force, when she'd assumed he'd been a marine, like her father and like Quinn and his brothers.

As the evening wore on, Clairy laid out everything, and she and Quinn debated what should and shouldn't be included. Clairy had experience dealing with vets and their families who believed everything was golden and should be put on display. When it came to his father, Quinn fell into that category. Fortunately, Clairy had success finessing him through the process, pointing out why certain things only detracted from his father's greatest accomplishments, negotiating with him when he stood his ground on a few things until they'd agreed on what would be used and what wouldn't.

Then they repacked the boxes—one with the items Clairy would keep, the rest with what Quinn would take with him when he left.

Which it was clearly time for him to do once the purpose for them getting together had wrapped up.

But despite her earlier bad reaction to the White House event, despite having passed nearly three hours in each other's company, the fact that Clairy had tried to resist it, she wasn't eager to usher out Quinn.

She should have been. But she wasn't. And before she'd figured out why, she said, "One more glass of tea?"

As if you aren't doing something you know you shouldn't do just because you're sticking with tea, she silently sneered at herself.

"I think I'm good, thanks."

"Would you rather have a beer? A glass of wine... now that we're done with work?"

She wanted to kick herself.

What's wrong with you?

But she knew what was wrong with her whether she wanted to admit it or not—she didn't want to see him go yet.

"No, thanks, I really am good," he repeated.

Maybe she didn't want him to go yet because she still had more questions about his father.

"I keep wondering why, with your dad being in the air force and you and your brothers wanting to follow in his footsteps, you all went into the marines," she said.

It was a last-ditch effort, but also something she *had* been wondering about and hadn't found an opportunity to ask.

It did the trick, because Quinn sat down on the sofa—and not just a perch on the edge to give her a quick answer. He sat at one end, his right elbow on the arm, his left arm resting along the top of the couch's back and his left calf propped on top of the opposite knee, all as if the offer of more to drink was an invitation to stay.

Which, of course, it had been.

Clairy sat in the other corner of the sofa to hear his answer, feeling a ridiculous amount of gladness that he'd accepted the veiled invitation and reassuring herself that what she'd just done was purely in the interest of getting to know each other.

Why else would the entire length of the sofa be separating them?

It couldn't be more innocent...

"I know. You'd think we all—or at least one of us—would have gone into the air force, wouldn't you?" Quinn said. "But none of us were interested in flying. I don't know whether Dad dying in a plane crash factored in for my brothers, but it did for me."

There had been no indication in any of the memorabilia that Reese Camden had died in a plane crash, so this was news to Clairy. Hearing it now, she assumed it was while he was in the service, so she said, "Was it wartime or peacetime when the plane crash happened?"

"He was a civilian when he died—he'd left the air force," Quinn said, as if he thought she knew. "He was in the air force from 1978 to 1986, but alive and well when he resigned—just after being awarded the Meritorious Service Medal that I brought you. He died two years later from a mechanical failure flying a private plane for the other branch of the Camden family—the Colorado Camdens. My great-grandfather Hector was H. J. Camden's brother."

"I knew there was some connection between your family and the Camden-Superstores Camdens. I just didn't know how."

"That's how. When my mom found out she was having triplets—with three-month-old Micah already on her hands—Dad decided he had to be around more than he could be if he stayed in the military. But he still needed a job and flying was what he wanted to do, so he became the other Camdens' private pilot. And ultimately that was how he went—at twenty-eight—flying a Camden plane," Quinn said, some sadness echoing in his voice.

"How old were you?"

"Not quite two. Micah was barely three—"

"You were two years old?" Clairy said, surprised. She recalled Quinn's comment the night before about not having a dad and her own curiosity about what he'd meant. Now that she thought more concretely about it, she realized that she didn't have an exact timetable for Quinn's family history. She'd been just a child herself and hadn't thought about the parents of other kids—she'd just assumed they had them. Including Quinn.

Trying to understand how she'd been so off base, she said, "I remember thinking that Ben was your dad until I was about eleven or twelve—I was throwing a fit about you being around so much and asked Mim why you didn't stay with your own father instead of always coming around after Mac. She told me Ben was your *grand*father, that your dad had died. But I didn't realize it had been so long before that. I took it as something that had just happened—"

"When I was thirteen or fourteen? Hardly."

"I remember trying to be a little nicer about you coming around for a while because I felt sorry for you—"

"I know that didn't last," Quinn said with a laugh.

"Well, no," she admitted somewhat contritely. "I figured you still had your grandfather around all the time, so you shouldn't be taking what little time I had with my father when he was here on leave…"

Clairy shook her head at her own cluelessness, readjusting her thinking to incorporate this new information. "I've always thought your dad was career military who died while he was in the service when you were older—definitely not when you were *two...*"

"I don't know what to tell you," Quinn said with a shrug at her misconceptions. "But you were just a kid—younger than me—and it wasn't as if you were ever at my house, or that I ever told you about my family or who was who. I can see where you could have thought Big Ben was my dad—for all intents and purposes, he was."

"So you didn't really ever even know your father," Clairy observed, putting some pieces together.

"I don't have any memory of him, no. Not even Micah does. When Dad died, we came here from Denver to live with Big Ben—"

"I also just assumed you were born in Merritt. I guess because you were here when I got here I thought you'd always been here."

"Nope. Dalton, Tanner and I were born in Colorado. My mom lived on base there when my dad was in the air force, and Denver is where the other Camdens were, too. When he resigned and went to work as their private pilot, we stayed there, in a suburb outside of the city."

"I really had it wrong."

"I guess you did," Quinn said, as if it didn't have any relevance to him.

"So no wonder you were hungry for a father figure."

He grimaced at that. "That makes it sound like Big Ben dropped the ball somehow, and after all he did for us, all he's been to us in place of a father, he definitely didn't do that," Quinn said, clearly making sure credit was given where credit was due.

But when he went on, it was in a confidential tone. "But for me…yeah, I guess I did want more than what my grandfather was. I love Big Ben. I'm grateful to him. I'd lay down my life for him. There's no better man. But he's a quiet, gentle guy. He was the sensitive influence in our lives—"

"Your mother wasn't the sensitive influence in your life?"

Quinn laughed. "No way!" he said, as if the idea of that was laughable. He didn't expand on it, though, but went on talking about his grandfather. "Big Ben was more our philosopher, our moral compass. And it was lucky we had him, believe me. But… I don't know… Maybe I had something to prove. I wanted a tough taskmaster to show that I could meet harder challenges, to mold me into something stronger, maybe. I'm not sure what the drive was. I just know that your old man fit the bill, that when I could meet his standards, I felt like I could do anything, like nothing could beat me, and that was the way I wanted to feel."

Clairy thought there was so much more in what he was saying that it opened her eyes to a view of a scared kid who had lost his father before he'd even known him, who had grown up with a sense of vulnerability that had probably come out of that loss even if he hadn't realized it. A scared kid who had believed that if he could make himself tough enough, he could truly feel safe. Just a kid who probably also wanted to shine especially bright for that father who wasn't there.

And it broke her heart. It made her realize all the more that little-boy Quinn wasn't at fault for her father ignoring her, that the blame for letting her down rested solely on Mac.

And it gave her a flush of guilt for resenting Quinn so much, even if that resentment *had* come out of her own family issues.

It also complicated things for her when Quinn seemed less a villain and more just another child with his own needs for a parent. When she saw things through his eyes and felt compassion for him.

Especially since that compassion opened the door for other emotions to come through. Emotions that weren't all negative. That softened the way she felt about him suddenly.

Not that she had *feelings* for him.

"I didn't understand then," she said quietly. "I just thought you were…*greedy*. That you were sucking up the time my father should have been spending with me, when you had your own father—or grandfather—to spend time with." She took a turn at shrugging. "So I was a jerk to you, too."

"Well, you weren't nice to me, that's for sure," he said without any real injury in his tone, as if he was merely cashing in on whatever culpability she was owning up to.

"I'm sorry?" she said in the form of a question, because she wasn't admitting she'd done anything wrong, just that she'd misconstrued some things in her own innocence.

"Is that supposed to be an apology?" he goaded, obviously unaware of the empathy he'd generated in her.

Clairy thought that was probably for the best, because she couldn't imagine that this man, of all men, would appreciate being felt sorry for. Even if it did put him in a better light with her.

"I *was* just a kid. And you were as obnoxious and mean to me as you could possibly have been," she reminded him. "So of the two of us, I'd say you still come out as the bigger jerk."

"Man, I can't catch a break with you no matter what," he lamented.

But the tone between them was light, teasing, when she muttered, "Let's just say it might get you a little closer to a break."

"Really…" he said, as if he saw possibilities in that, his own voice laced with interest.

"Not too close," she returned, not wanting to admit to too much.

"I'll have to keep working on it," he promised in a quieter, more intimate tone.

Their gazes stayed steadily connected for a moment before Quinn broke the connection.

"I should go. It's getting late," he said, standing.

Clairy didn't argue this time. She just stood up, too, taking the box nearest to her that held items she'd rejected. "I'll help you get some of this out," she said, even though he was leaving with less than he'd carried in and didn't need the help. But she told herself the same thing she'd told herself the previous evening—that she could use the fresh air.

Quinn put the two remaining boxes on top of each other and carried them under one arm so he still had a free hand to open her front door, then the screen door, and hold it for her.

"So," she said as she stepped onto the porch with him and they headed for his truck, "have you heard yet that your old friend Brad Nelan asked my friend Marabeth Hawn to marry him?"

"Brad and I usually see each other when I'm here, but we don't keep up in between. I didn't even know he was seeing Marabeth until he and I had breakfast this morning and he told me."

"Well, we can't get into the library again tomorrow because of the raccoons—apparently, there are more of them than the cleaning crew saw and they're a wily bunch—so I thought I'd use the day to put together an engagement barbecue for tomorrow night… Did Brad tell you that?"

"He did."

"Did he invite you?"

"He did. Is that all right?"

"Sure. That's why I'm asking, because if he didn't, I would." Not for any reason except that he was Brad Nelan's friend, Clairy told herself.

"Then it's okay if I come?" Quinn asked when they reached his truck and he set his two boxes on the passenger seat, turning to take the third box from her.

In doing that, his big hands brushed her forearms where they were wrapped around the box.

It was nothing. Brief, scant contact. And yet it sent a ripple of something charged through her, stealing her attention from his question.

And, apparently, her lack of reply caused him to think the lack of speed in answering meant she didn't want him to come, because, before she said anything, he said, "I know that's not library-memorial work. If my coming crosses a boundary—"

"No," she said too quickly. She consciously cut back on her enthusiasm, then insisted, "Of course you should come. Like I said, I was about to invite you. You're Brad's friend."

"Still…" Quinn allowed, giving her an out.

"Definitely come," she responded, clasping her

arms around herself to stop the lingering sensation of that brush of his hands.

He deposited that last box in the truck and closed the door, and when he turned back to her, he was somehow standing closer than she'd anticipated.

She considered taking a step back.

But she didn't.

"Will you have a date?" he asked out of the blue.

That caused Clairy to laugh. "I don't know who I would have a date with," she said to the absurdity of the idea.

But then she sobered when it occurred to her that Quinn might be asking because he wanted to bring one.

"You can, if you want…"

Oh, there was no gusto at all in that offer.

But Quinn smiled a thoughtful smile, his eyes on hers, and said, "How about if we're each other's?"

Dates?

That seemed like a really bad idea.

And still, she replied, "Okay."

He nodded, his expression satisfied and something else as he went on looking down at her. "Good," he almost whispered, as if it was a secret.

And something about that just-between-them hushed voice caused kissing to pop into Clairy's mind for the second night in a row.

Which was silly, she told herself, because, of course, kissing wasn't going to happen.

Until Quinn leaned forward just enough to make it happen. His mouth was suddenly on hers ever so lightly, his lips parted ever so slightly, extending an invitation of his own.

That she accepted by kissing him back.

With her eyes closed, her head tilted even more and her lips parted, too. Which encouraged him to deepen the kiss, to take away all tentativeness and make it real.

His big hands came to her upper arms to hold and caress them and send stronger, more vibrant currents all through her. She didn't unclasp her arms from around her middle, using them to provide herself with a small sense that she still had some control.

His lips were smooth. His breath against her skin was warm. Even that sexy stubble was soft. And he was such a good kisser...

Good enough that she could have gone on kissing him all night long.

Which meant that even though it was a fairly lengthy kiss, it still seemed way too short when Quinn drew it to a close and straightened up.

His eyes came to hers again with what almost looked like awe in them.

He didn't apologize, as she thought he might. He didn't ask if it was all right that he'd kissed her. He just left that kiss between them, squeezed her arms once and took away his hands.

"Tomorrow night," he said then. "I'm happy to come early and help if you can use me."

An image of *using* him flashed through her mind at that offer, but Clairy dodged it in a hurry.

"It's just a barbecue. It won't be fancy," she answered, finally taking a few steps backward, onto the lawn.

"Just let me know," he said as he went around to the driver's side and got behind the wheel, turning on the engine while Clairy merely nodded in response.

All as if he hadn't just kissed her.

And as much as she played with the thought of telling him he shouldn't have, of acting incensed and outraged, of letting him know he'd better not ever do it again, she just took one more step backward and waved weakly to send him away.

Because while something inside her shouted that Quinn Camden was no one she should be canoodling with, kissing him again was all she could think about.

Chapter Five

Clairy was up at dawn on Wednesday. It helped that many of the guests invited to the impromptu engagement party that she was throwing for Marabeth had insisted on pitching in, but still, Clairy had a jam-packed day ahead of her.

The weather couldn't have been better for an outdoor party—sunny and warm but not too hot—so there was no worry about that.

Mim's green thumb had already made the sprawling backyard a lush venue. Marabeth's aunt owned the local barbecue restaurant and was catering. Marabeth's uncle had the best cheesecake recipe in town and had volunteered to provide cheesecakes for dessert, claiming he wanted the chance to show off.

Her three bridesmaids had wanted to contribute, so they were supplying drinks—alcoholic and non. One of the groomsmen was in a band and was eager to provide music. And the wife of the best man wanted to do an appetizer platter.

Clairy was doing two more of those, but they were at the bottom of a long list of things that had to be done before. She needed to shop for the ingredients for those other appetizers along with decorations, disposable plates, glasses, napkins, silverware, serving utensils and tablecloths.

She needed to be home in time to receive delivery of the tables and chairs she'd rented, as well as the flower arrangement she'd ordered to adorn the serving table, and the Congratulations On Your Engagement banner and helium-filled balloons.

She had to arrange all the tables and chairs, set everything out and decorate before the appetizers could be made. Then she would need to shower, dress and do her hair and makeup.

With all of that on her to-do list and details galore also running through her head, it seemed as if there wouldn't be any room for thoughts of Quinn.

And yet he was there between every line on her list, there between each errand she ran and there without interruption as she worked alone in the quiet of the backyard that afternoon.

He'd done the impossible—talking about what had caused him to pursue her father as his mentor had opened up a soft spot in her for the little father-less boy he'd been.

He'd let her see that he'd craved a father's attention as much as she had. Maybe even more.

They'd both had grandfathers in their lives—hers as gruff as her father and offering not much more of a paternal relationship than the General, while Quinn had had a closer bond with his. But still, hurt by the General's rejections and disregard for her, Clairy had merely sought refuge in her bedroom to lick her wounds. Quinn, on the other hand—and even *with* comfort from his grandfather—had toughed it out with the General. He'd taken Mac's harshest treatment in order to have contact with him, time with him.

Granted, she hadn't had that option because her father had ordered her to go away whenever she'd tried to do anything with him, or with him and Quinn. But she'd spied on enough of Quinn's training to have witnessed just how exacting it had been and wondered why he just didn't go home and never come back, why he'd kept coming back day after day, visit after visit.

In her years of counseling family members left behind by veterans they'd lost, Clairy had seen more than a fair share of kids who had longed for that lost parent and the attention they would have received from them to somehow be replaced, for that hole in their lives to be filled.

She'd seen misbehavior and acting out in a destructive way. She'd seen kids who tried too hard to please, sometimes to the point of courting danger. She'd seen kids trying to excel in order to be noticed—to their benefit when the achievements stacked up, to their emotional detriment if they failed again and again.

And not once had she pieced together that Quinn might have been one of those kids. But now she was beginning to think that he was.

Fortunately for him, he'd fallen into the group of stacking up achievements rather than failures, and for his sake, she was glad. But her heart still went out to the little fatherless boy who had felt compelled to take the worst the General had to offer.

And, yes, that had made something shift in her—it had raised compassion for him for the first time, opening up that soft spot she'd recognized last night.

But was that what had led to that kiss?

Going into the evening with him, she'd thought that she'd had control over that. She'd been sure it wouldn't even cross her mind the way it had at the end of Monday night.

Instead, rather than merely thinking about kissing, it had happened. And she definitely hadn't been thinking of him as a little fatherless boy when it had.

But what if compassion and that soft spot for him had paved the way for more?

For attraction she didn't want to admit to. Attraction she had to be careful with.

After all, what had driven him to come between her and her father—and despite the fact that she was coming to see more and more that her father bore most of the blame—didn't excuse Quinn of everything, she thought as she spread tablecloths on all the tables.

Yes, she might have discovered she could forgive the actions of the very young Quinn, but there had also been spite and meanness in the way teenage Quinn had treated her, and for that he didn't get a free pass.

In fact, she knew she should be extra cautious because how much of that mean, spiteful, arrogant, heartless teenager might have carried over into the man?

"You should have thought about that last night before you kissed him. It might have stopped you," she told herself.

But would anything have stopped her?

Something needed to, she decided, even though rather than regretting that kiss, she hadn't been able to *stop* thinking about it since it had happened. Any more than she'd been able to keep from wanting to do it again.

And she'd already been thinking about him constantly. Falling asleep every night picturing him, fantasizing about him. On top of the fact that spending hours and hours with him still didn't seem like enough.

But what if the spiteful, mean, arrogant teenager

hadn't stuck with grown-up Quinn and the man he'd become was not only a feast for the eyes, but also a genuinely good guy underneath it—the way Marabeth thought Brad had turned out?

Clairy wasn't quite sure where that notion had come from as she opened folding chairs around the tables, but she knew that thinking about that possibility certainly wasn't a good way to tamp down on an attraction to Quinn! It wouldn't leave much to resist, would it?

When she really considered the likelihood of such a drastic change in him, though, she couldn't actually believe it. Not when she recalled just how badly he'd treated her.

And none of it mattered, anyway, because it wasn't as if he was a prospect for a relationship, she reasoned as she finished setting up the serving table and went for the ladder in order to string up the banner and balloons.

A relationship?

Was that what these thoughts were inching toward?

"Oh, Clairy..." she said to herself with a sigh. "You can't be entertaining the slightest idea of a relationship—not now and not with Quinn Camden."

But the very outlandishness of that possibility made it occur to her that all of these feelings could very well be a postdivorce ripple.

She'd also done marriage and divorce counseling

for veterans, for the spouses of veterans. And she'd seen divorce among friends. She knew there were many things that could show up in the aftermath of a split, including a desire to fill the gap with a new person, a new romance, a new relationship.

No, she wasn't aware of feeling any of that, but that didn't necessarily mean it wasn't simmering somewhere in her subconscious.

Especially when her marriage had turned into a situation so similar to her childhood and she'd found herself overlooked and inconsequential again.

That had to be factoring in, she realized.

Here she was, coming out of a divorce from a man who had barely been aware of her for almost the entirety of their marriage, and she was now spending time with someone who was drop-dead gorgeous and was paying attention to her, putting effort into getting to know her and clearly not overlooking her.

No matter what kind of a jerk he'd once been.

All she needed to do was ride out what was nothing more than the first postdivorce phase and stop making it a big deal.

By the time the outside was ready for guests and she'd moved into the kitchen to make hors d'oeuvres, she had herself convinced that was all that was going on with her and she didn't need to worry about whatever she was feeling toward Quinn.

And not only was this merely phase one, she decided as she hollowed out cherry peppers and stuffed them with cream cheese and prosciutto, this whole thing with him had a short shelf life because—like her father—Quinn being here was only a temporary thing. A visit on leave.

After which he would return to duty, her life would go on, and that would be that.

So whether or not she'd forgiven him or found compassion for him, whether or not she had a soft spot for him, whether or not he'd evolved into the most wonderful man on earth, it didn't make any difference. It wasn't even of any consequence if she was fixating on him a little for the moment—it was probably just therapeutic.

And if she needed something to keep her grounded in reality, she reminded herself of the one thing she did know about Quinn—he was military through and through. Like her father. Which meant that he was devoted to the marines in a way he would never be as devoted to anything or anyone else.

It was what she'd suffered as a kid, what she'd blamed—as much as she'd blamed Quinn—for not having all she should have had with the General. It was what she'd experienced again in her marriage, despite the fact that Jared was a civilian. He'd been devoted to something other than her, too. And that had confirmed in spades that she didn't ever want to be in any other relationship where she was second fiddle—not to the military or anything else.

Twice was enough.

As she finished the second appetizer tray of fresh vegetables with a spicy Southwestern vegetable dip to go along with them, she felt as if what was happening when it came to Quinn was more containable and less worrisome.

So she was going to worry less about it and contain it more.

And yet still, as she checked the time and rushed upstairs to shower and get ready for the party, she couldn't stop thinking about Quinn.

She couldn't stop wanting to be with him.

And there she was, with the hope that he might kiss her again causing a flash of excitement to run through her.

"It's just phase one and it will pass," she reassured herself.

But before it did, should she or shouldn't she indulge?

Everyone seemed to have a great time at the engagement party. The food was a big hit, there were toasts and congratulation speeches galore, sing-alongs with the band and so many engagement gifts that they filled the back seat when they were all loaded into Marabeth's car.

Marabeth's aunt cleaned up all the barbecue paraphernalia she'd brought with the food. Her uncle left Clairy half a cheesecake, but otherwise took away everything else he'd provided.

Marabeth's cousin owned the rental shop where the tables and chairs had come from, and before leaving, Maxwell folded them, loaded everything into the back of his truck and took them away.

Marabeth wanted the balloons. The band packed their own gear and in the process dislodged the banner, which Marabeth also took as a memento. Ultimately, Clairy was left with a lot of full trash bags and some cleaning to do when everyone cleared out.

Everyone except Quinn.

Clairy thought that might have been as part of his suggestion the previous evening that they attend the party as each other's dates. There hadn't been much of tonight that had even given them the opportunity to speak to each other, but maybe he still felt obliged—in his role as her date—to insist on staying to help clean up.

Nothing she said could dissuade him, so she finally gave in.

As Clairy took in the last of the food, Quinn carried all the trash bags out to the curb for Thursday's pickup.

Then he joined her in the kitchen.

But rather than addressing the dishes in the sink or what littered the kitchen table, Clairy said, "I can do the rest of this in the morning. I'm ready to take off these shoes and have my piece of cheesecake—want some?"

She was still on the fence about whether or not to

indulge in any more of the things she was fantasizing about when it came to Quinn. But what she was sure of was that after an entire evening of just being two ships passing in the night, she wasn't nearly as ready to say goodbye to him as she had been to everyone else.

In fact, when she'd been offered that half a cheesecake, she'd said yes mainly as bait, with just this moment in mind.

"Sounds good—I didn't get around to dessert, either," Quinn answered, leaving her with no clue whether he wanted a few more minutes with her, too, or just the cheesecake.

But Clairy remained glad he was there as she turned off the backyard lights and went to the refrigerator.

"It's still so warm out," she said. "How about if we sit on the front porch?"

"Sure," he agreed.

Clairy cut two pieces of super-creamy cheesecake, ladled raspberry puree over the tops and added a spoonful of fresh berries and mint to them.

"Spoons or forks, and where do I find them?" Quinn inquired.

"Spoons, I think, so we don't lose any of this sauce I've been hearing about all night. And they're in that drawer next to the fridge," she instructed, taking a dessert plate in each hand as Quinn opened the drawer and retrieved utensils.

Clairy led him from the kitchen to the front of the house. While she kicked off her sandals at the foot of the stairs, Quinn opened the screen door.

"There's only the swing, but it's big enough for both of us," she said, handing him a slice of cheese-cake and accepting the spoon he traded it for once they were outside.

Then Clairy went to the padded swing hanging at one end of the porch.

"Oh, that feels good," she moaned in more rapture than was called for by merely getting off her feet, making Quinn grin a slightly ribald grin as he propped one hip on the railing nearby.

"Don't you want to sit down?" she asked.

"I'm fine," he said, making her wonder if he wanted to keep some space between them.

If that was the purpose, it was slightly disheartening to her.

But there was compensation in the fact that they weren't sitting side by side: she got to look at him.

He was dressed in a pair of gray slacks tonight, with a lighter gray shirt, the long sleeves rolled up past his forearms.

She liked seeing him in civvies. He might not look quite as rugged as he did in everything else, but there was no less appeal in the more refined version. And the well-groomed scruff kept him from looking too polished.

Since she had the swing to herself, she pivoted slightly on the seat so the full view was unhampered.

Tonight she'd chosen to wear a flowered sundress with a square-cut neckline so wide it barely covered her shoulders and only allowed for a built-in bra in the tight-fitting bodice that attached to a large circle skirt.

Not only was there a considerable amount of fabric forming the circle, but the skirt also hit just above her ankles. She draped it demurely over her legs and feet when she tucked them under one hip.

Once she was settled, she discovered Quinn watching her. Until she caught him—then he averted his gaze to his plate and tasted the cheesecake.

"Woo, old Manuel has reason to brag about this," Quinn commented.

"He told me when he offered to bring dessert that his cheesecake recipe is the best in the state—maybe in the country or the whole world," Clairy explained with some humor, quoting the older man's own words.

"I think he might be right," Quinn said, going in for another spoonful as Clairy began to eat hers.

"The sauce, too," she said with a mock swoon at the sweet-tangy puree. "He said I'd be sorry if I didn't let him bring that to put over the cheesecakes and he wasn't kidding."

As they went on relishing the treat, Quinn said, "It was a nice party."

"It seemed like everyone had a pretty good time."

"Seemed that way to me, too. How 'bout you? Did you enjoy it?"

"I did," Clairy said. "Did you?"

"I liked catching up with people I haven't seen in years. Seemed like you were getting bombarded with the same couple of questions I was, though, about what you've been up to since you left Merritt—that got a little old."

"Oh, yeah!" Clairy confirmed vigorously. "Only it's common knowledge that I'm back after getting divorced, so they were coming at you in a different tone than they were coming at me. You were getting the tell-me-about-your-adventures tone, and I was getting a whole lot of poor-Clairy stuff or fishing for dirt."

"Yeah, I heard that whenever I was in earshot of you," he replied, commiserating with her.

And he'd been within earshot most of the evening because it had almost seemed as if he was trying to get to her side the whole night.

Or was she just imagining that?

Regardless, he hadn't been too successful. He'd been the person everyone wanted to talk to, and most of the time she'd seen him headed for her, someone had waylaid him.

Although thinking about that reminded Clairy of when he had made it to her side. "Thanks for those two assists with Mrs. Rayburn. She was determined to get something juicy out of me."

Elsa Rayburn was the elderly town gossip, and on the two occasions she'd been grilling Clairy, Quinn had prematurely broken off his own nearby conversations and come to her rescue.

"I was trying for that third time, but I think she sent in Mr. Rayburn to block me, because that old bugger either couldn't hear me trying to excuse myself or just ignored me and kept talking—"

"His hearing is just fine—he probably had been given orders to nab you and not let you go."

"Well, he did a good job—he literally had me cornered. I would have had to knock him down to pass him," Quinn said with a laugh. "So I was stuck listening to his army reserve stories for half an hour."

"Marabeth saved me from that third one or I might still be stuck," Clairy said, laughing, too. "Thank goodness the Rayburns wore out early and left!"

They'd both finished their dessert and Clairy motioned with her dish. "Want a second piece of cheesecake?"

"No. It's good, but rich—one is enough," Quinn said.

If only that was true of that kiss last night…

Maybe it would be if you'd just stop thinking about it! Clairy chastised herself.

Pushing off the porch railing, Quinn came to take her plate. He set both of the small dishes on a small table near the front door.

Clairy was a little afraid he was segueing to leave,

but then he turned back to her. Retracing his steps, he joined her on the swing. He angled in her direction, one arm resting atop the swing's back just behind the cap sleeve that covered her left shoulder.

Glad he hadn't been gearing up to go home yet—and not unhappy to have him seem to relax more by sitting with her even though it made not thinking about kissing him again impossible—she relaxed a bit more, too.

But when she did it created a minor problem—in order to keep her hair contained and off her neck tonight, she'd twisted the thick waves into a knot in back and held it there with a chopstick-like brass comb. As she leaned back, that brass comb got lodged in the chain holding up her side of the swing.

"Uh-oh… I'm stuck…" she said, forced to pull the comb from the knot and chain at once and leaving her hair to spill.

Without anything coy in mind, when her hair came out of the knot, she shook her head to loosen the thick strands so they could fall free.

That done, for a second time she caught Quinn steadfastly watching her.

But once more, the instant she noticed it, he stopped abruptly.

"Am I wrong or are you not a hundred percent thrilled that your friend is marrying mine?" he asked without preamble.

That was not such a light topic…

Was she going to admit to the truth or not?

She hadn't decided when he added, "I thought there was a little anti-Brad under the surface when you asked if I knew they were engaged last night and told me about the party. Then tonight—don't get me wrong, you were the perfect hostess—I still thought there might be a whiff of you liking Marabeth better than Brad. Even your toast was slanted toward Marabeth, with barely a mention of him."

"Marabeth is my best friend, so I do like her better. Brad is…just the guy she's marrying," she hedged.

She'd thought her voice had been completely neutral, the same way she'd thought she'd covered up her dislike of Brad all evening. But something about what she said caused Quinn to frown and shake his head, as if he saw through her and wasn't going to let this slide.

"You still don't like him," Quinn mused. He stalled for a moment and then said, "I was recently reminded of an incident…" He was silent again, as if he was treading lightly into this subject. "That day in the cafeteria when you tried to persuade me to stay away from Mac."

So he remembered it.

Clairy had wondered.

"Is Brad on your hate list, too? For backing me up?" Quinn asked.

"My *hate list*? I don't have a hate list."

"You do—I'm at the top of it, and unless I'm mistaken..." he said, as if he was putting things together as he spoke. "Is Brad next on the list?"

Clairy rolled her eyes as if he was delusional.

But that didn't deter him, either. "You have some reason for being down on him, too—Tanner reminded me that he and Brad were there when it all went down, that I gave you a hard time and that Brad piled on."

"Your brother didn't," she said, apropos of nothing except that she'd always given Tanner Camden some amnesty for that and it seemed worth noting.

"But Brad was almost as bad as I was," Quinn said, still piecing things together.

Clairy let silence, and the stiffness of her spine, speak for her while she thought again of why she should resist any attraction she might have to Quinn—phase one of her postdivorce life or not.

"Looking back, that whole deal was pretty bad, wasn't it? And it was worse when Brad got into it. It pitted you against both of us. And you were younger and outnumbered, and it was ugly and only got uglier when Brad chimed in and we started to one-up each other on the smart-ass snarkiness."

And clearly, Quinn didn't recall it without working at it, while it was one of the worst moments of her life and something she'd never forgotten.

Clairy only answered with an arch of her eyebrows.

"So Brad is second on the hate list," Quinn concluded. "And now he's marrying your best friend, and you've moved back to town, and that means that to be in Marabeth's life again, Brad will be in yours... You aren't thrilled with that."

"I'm more worried about the kind of person who will be Marabeth's husband," Clairy said frankly.

"O-o-h...that's even worse than you just not liking him," Quinn said, as if light was dawning. "You think she's marrying someone who showed a bad side of himself to you, and you're afraid that's how he could end up treating Marabeth when she's married to him."

"I was where Marabeth is now—freshly courted, newly engaged... It's great. Everything is rosy. But I was also married for years and I know what can happen when the bloom is off the rose. If the person you marry was different before meeting you, before they were on their best behavior and putting their best foot forward for you, that's the person they become again."

"Ouch!" he said, as if she was referring to him.

And certainly he was included in what she was leery of, and on the lookout for, because she wasn't convinced that underneath his current agreeable behavior, that mean, insensitive beast wasn't just waiting to come out again.

"Does Marabeth know where you stand?" he asked then.

"She says Brad grew out of that teenage big-man stuff, that he isn't the same person."

"You don't believe it?"

"I'm skeptical," Clairy said honestly.

"I'm sorry to hear that," Quinn said, as if he'd just taken a bit of a blow himself. "That has to mean you don't have much faith that I grew out of that stuff, either."

"Are you less driven than you were? Less bound and determined to go after what you want at any cost? If there's an obstacle in your way, is there anything you won't do to trample over it?"

"Yes and no—it depends on the circumstances now. Not letting anything stand in my way still sums me up as a marine. It's what's gotten me where I am, what makes me good at what I do. But I've learned that it isn't always the way to handle things—in fact, I've just lately seen that same philosophy in someone else go really wrong and learned a whole new lesson when it comes to that."

His voice had gone quiet at the end, into that mysterious tone he'd used when he'd told her that he knew some things now that he hadn't known before.

To Clairy, it seemed as if his mind had wandered into more than answering her questions. But he didn't give her a chance to delve into it before he came back to the moment and went on. "And, yes, that's all a part of me because my mother wouldn't have it any other way. It was how my brothers and I got what we wanted—it was at the core of your father, too."

"Who just added to it in you," Clairy said fatalistically. "It didn't make him a nice guy, either. Or someone really successful at relationships—especially with women."

Quinn closed his eyes, his brows arched, and Clairy wasn't sure what button she'd pushed, but it seemed as if she'd pushed one. He appeared to have contained it, though, when he opened his eyes again. "No argument—your dad didn't die with a lot of friends," he said morosely, as if that admission brought some kind of remorse to him personally. "And he also didn't have a woman in his life...well, except you and Mim."

"And it couldn't be said that we were very much in his life," Clairy pointed out.

But rather than go on, she returned to what he'd said tonight, and last night, too, in reference to his mother—actually, what he'd also said on Monday night, when Clairy had aired her complaints against him and he'd said that going after what he wanted the way he had was a result of being raised by Raina Camden.

"Did your mother want you to be like the General?"

"My mother didn't know much about Mac, so it wasn't that she aimed me in his direction hoping I'd end up like him—although when she found out that I was hounding him to teach me to be a marine, she was all in favor of that because anything I wouldn't let up on got her approval. My mother wanted strong sons and she had her own method of getting us there."

His mother had encouraged her son to hound an adult for his attention?

That seemed odd to Clairy. "Her own method..." she repeated, trying to understand.

"I told you my father died piloting a private plane for the other side of the Camden family—"

"The Superstore Camdens."

"And like I said, the Superstore Camdens came from H. J. Camden, my great-grandfather Hector's brother. Not only did my mother hold my father's death against the other Camdens, but she also took an old family story about the Superstores being Hector's original idea and decided that if it was Hector's idea, he should have been in line for half of what the other Camdens made with that idea."

"It seems like there could be something to that... You don't think he should have?" she asked, interpreting Quinn's tone.

He shrugged. "It's one point of view, I guess, but she was the only one of my family who ever held it. She could never get Hector—when he was alive—or Big Ben or my dad on board with it, or with going after the other Camdens for what she thought was owed us all. And because they wouldn't fight for it, to her, that made them weak. She loved them, but she thought they let themselves be doormats to the other Camdens, and it made her hell-bent on not letting her sons be like that."

"And she accomplished that how?" Clairy asked, fearing something harsh.

Quinn must have seen that, because he chuckled wryly, then said, "She didn't do anything bad—she was a good mom, but she was a strong woman and she had a game plan to make her sons strong, too."

"And the game plan?"

"She made us compete with each other over everything. With four boys, that meant some fierce competition—over who got the last biscuit when more than one of us wanted it, over who got to choose what we watched on TV, over who had to do the worst chores. Every single thing that involved more than one of us became a contest."

"How?" Clairy asked.

"She set up obstacles we had to overcome or ways to earn what we wanted or to prove we wanted it most, and whoever came out on top won out. And if she had so much as an inkling that we'd backed down from any challenge—at home or anywhere else—we were in more trouble with her than whenever there was a report of any one of us being too aggressive."

"She wanted you to be aggressive?"

"Yep. The more aggressive, the better," Quinn confirmed. "To her, that showed strength, and strength was what she wanted to see in us."

"So if you wanted my father's attention, you'd

been taught to do whatever you had to do to get it...
and it was something that made your mother proud?"

"Yes and yes. But there are a couple of things I'm
getting at," he said, as if he didn't want to go into
any more of this at the cost of why he was laying
that groundwork. "Like I told you before, as a kid,
I wanted Mac to take me under his wing and I just
did what I thought I was supposed to do—anything
it took to get what I wanted. By the time I was a
teenager...well, we've already established that that
time of life, on top of living up to my mom's expectations, didn't make me a nice guy. But I *did* grow
up, and now I know when to use my powers for good
and when to put them on the shelf," he said, injecting
some humor into a serious subject.

Then he went back to what had gotten them into
this conversation. "When it comes to Brad and that
day with you that put him on your hate list, he was
just doing the obnoxious-teenage-boy thing and following my lead—he was jumping on my obnoxious,
bad-behavior bandwagon because that's what teenage
boys do to show off and prove they're tough and cool
and all that teenage stuff. Sure, sometimes it sticks
with some guys who never grow up, but that isn't me
and it isn't Brad, so I know you don't have to worry
about what kind of husband he'll make Marabeth."

That had been a long and winding road to make
his point, and it had said more about Quinn than it

had about Brad, so Clairy just responded, "I hope you're right."

"I know I am," Quinn added confidently. "Brad isn't just on his best behavior and putting his best foot forward. What you see of him now is what he honestly is now—grown up and a good guy. He's a veterinarian, for crying out loud—he delivers puppies and kittens."

"And you?" she challenged, reserving judgment on her friend's fiancé and hoping her fears were as unfounded as Quinn thought they were.

"I have never delivered puppies or kittens. I did deliver a human baby once—under combat fire in a small village while my unit held off insurgents, if that gets me any leniency."

"Or are you just on your best behavior and putting your best foot forward for now?"

"If I was aiming for pulling the wool over your eyes, wouldn't I be swearing to you that I never tap into that part of me that burned you when we were kids?" he reasoned. "Instead, I've been honest. I haven't lied or pretended that I *don't* ever tap into that part of me. What I'm telling you is that when it's necessary, when it's called for, I do use it, but *not* otherwise, because I did grow up."

"Meaning that you can accept that you don't always get what you want?" she said, doubt in her voice.

"Yes," he answered. "Despite what my mother

taught me, I know when *not* to trample over people to get what I want, no matter how bad I want it."

"And you can just do that—set aside what your mother *ingrained* in you? What works for you? What's gotten you what you want since you were a little kid?" Clairy said dubiously.

"H. J. Camden was an underhanded, ruthless cut-throat. There wasn't an ethical bone in his body and that's why my great-grandfather didn't want anything to do with the building of the empire that those tactics created. Am I a hard-nosed marine when I need to be? Absolutely. Has my personal life suffered from the single-mindedness I've had when it comes to my career?" His eyebrows arched again, this time with something that looked like remorse. "It has—but in the form of neglect, not because of anything like what I did to land on your hate list. But the thing is, Clairy, time has taught me that being a marine is more than I thought it was as a kid, more than using what my mother *ingrained* in me. I guess you could say that the marines took what she trained me to be, what Mac trained me to be, and added the code of values that were lacking in my teenage brain—"

"Your mother didn't give you values?"

"Sure, the basics—don't lie, cheat or steal. Big Ben was our moral compass, but when you're a kid and strength, persistence and never backing down no matter what are first and foremost to your mother and only parent... Well, as a kid I saw the other things as...fluid, I guess you could say."

"The marines taught you to back down?" she challenged.

"It was in the marines that I was taught and held to higher standards. Where I had to learn there was more value in earning respect than in getting what I wanted. It was where I had to learn about uncompromising integrity and unselfishness. Where I had to learn that achievements needed to come with honor, that honor was everything. So, yeah, now I *can* just set aside what my mother *ingrained* in me as a kid— what I was when you knew me before—to be the man the marines made."

He inclined his head slightly as he admitted, "Sometimes it's tough. But that's usually when it's the most important..."

Clairy couldn't deny the ring of truth to what he said, or the conviction in his voice, so she decided to let up on him. It also occurred to her that—like the timing of his father's death—the way Quinn had been raised was something she hadn't known about and it explained his actions, giving her a more complete picture of what had gone into making him who he was.

He sighed then and said, "How did we go from partying to all that?"

"You started it," she accused justifiably, since he'd initiated the talk about her not liking Marabeth's fiancé.

"I did, didn't I? Let's go back... It was a nice party."

Clairy laughed and repeated her earlier answer. "It seemed like everyone had a pretty good time."

"Seemed that way to me, too." But after that, he went on in a more serious, intimate tone. "I didn't get the chance to tell you how great you look."

The compliment might have been a little late, but she was still happy to have it from him. So much so that it was impossible for her not to smile. "Thanks, but I have to be the worse for wear by now," she said.

"No, you still look great," he assured her in a way that seemed as if he genuinely thought so, his gaze more intent on her face than it had been as they were talking. "I keep going back through my memories of you years ago. You were kind of a gawky, geeky-looking redhead then—"

With blotchy, pale skin that she was abundantly grateful to have outgrown.

But she didn't say that. Interrupting him, she said sarcastically, "Thanks so much."

"You were kind of a gawky, geeky-looking red-headed kid," he began again, "but growing up gets the credit for improving on that, too. I couldn't keep my eyes off you tonight." Then he tempered the appreciation with a crooked smile and said, "From Saturday to this, definitely an improvement."

"I wasn't expecting company Saturday. I was

packing and unpacking boxes. What do *you* wear to do that?"

"Full dress blues," he lied.

Clairy laughed, then found a way to return the compliment. "It was strange to see you in civvies. But you do them justice."

So much justice…

"I feel okay in jeans, but this kind of thing is like wearing someone else's clothes. Maybe because these *are* someone else's clothes, since I borrowed them from Tanner. But still…" he said, not taking the flattery too seriously. Then he returned to talking about the party. "My only gripe with tonight was that I didn't get any time with you. I kept trying, but Mr. Rayburn wasn't the only interception—there was one after another."

So she hadn't been imagining that he'd made attempts to touch base with her all night.

"Did you need something?" she asked, playing innocent.

"To say hello, to tell you how great you looked, to just have a minute with you."

Their previous conversation had done much to quell her thoughts of kissing him last night and repeating it tonight. But hearing him say that was all it took to bring back those thoughts.

"So you didn't just stay to take out the trash and have cheesecake?"

"That should have been why. But it isn't…" he

said, as if something had gotten the better of other intentions.

Between the two of them, Clairy realized that he was being more straightforward than she was and decided he might have earned some of that from her, so she said, "Whatever the reason, I'm glad you stayed."

He smiled and his oh-so-handsome face relaxed into a pleased expression. "Wow, you said that out loud."

"Did I?" Clairy said in mock surprise.

He laughed. "Maybe I just imagined it. Don't worry, I won't hold you to it," he teased.

So much for being straightforward with him. It just wasn't easy for her to admit or accept that when it came to him, things she was thinking, feeling and wanting were heading in directions she'd never thought possible.

"Isn't this strange for you, too?" she asked quietly, all joking aside. "You didn't like me any better than I liked you."

"And now things are changing," he said, moving his hand from where it was resting on the swing's back to take a strand of her hair between two fingers. "It's definitely strange," he confirmed with some confusion and awe in his tone. "But it's happening…"

Was he resolved to that? Giving in to it?

Was she?

Clairy didn't know. Or give it much more thought as he leaned in to kiss her.

She just instinctively responded to the kiss she'd been longing for, the kiss that made her feel as if the last twenty-four hours had no purpose but to get her back to that.

Just phase one, she told herself as the kiss almost instantly evolved to where they'd left off the night before—lips were parted and every moment deepened it.

Had she ever liked kissing anyone as much as she liked it with him? she wondered, astonished and swept away by how good he was at it, by just how much she did like it.

His other hand rose to the side of her face as mouths opened wider and the kiss took a detour into something even sexier, something erotic. Something that gave her goose bumps...

She placed both palms on his chest. The chest that looked so phenomenal in the tight T-shirts he usually wore, the chest that felt even better—strapping, brawny, solid.

Then his broad shoulders and his biceps came to mind, and on their own, her hands followed that same course, upward to his shoulders, down again to those biceps, where she dug her fingers in, testing the power there.

And every inch of that path made her sizzle even more inside, amping up what was already mounting between them.

Until a car drove by, reminding Clairy that they

were on her front porch, in plain view. And this had become far, far more than a kiss suitable for all audience members.

Her next thought was that maybe she should take Quinn inside to continue it.

But was she ready for the message that could send? *Yes!*

But, no, not really...

Still, she didn't want this to end. She wanted hours and hours of just kissing him until she couldn't kiss him anymore.

Except the car had pulled into the driveway of the house next door and the engine had been turned off.

Hating herself for it, she forced her hands up those glorious biceps and over his shoulders again, drawing them down to his chest, where she pushed against him just enough to let him know it was time to stop.

He got the message, because a small groan of complaint came from his throat as he put the kiss in Reverse until she lost his mouth altogether.

"I know... Neighbors," he grumbled.

Clairy eased away, and he took his hand from her face, his other hand out of her hair and added a few more inches of distance himself.

"I should probably get going, anyway," he grumbled. "It's late..."

"And we should be able to get into the library tomorrow, so I thought we should get to work going through my father's things—"

Clairy had no idea why that brought a fleeting, but very dark, frown to Quinn's face before he nodded somberly and said, "Mac told me where to look for things in your attic. We'll need to do that, and there are other things he's given me, things I cleaned out of his office and house in Jacksonville..."

"We can take it all to the library, go through it, sort it, spread it out there," Clairy said, fighting to pay any attention to that subject, when what she wanted to do was kiss Quinn again, even though her neighbor was taking his sweet time at his curbside mailbox, going through his mail there while really sneaking peeks at them.

"Okay," Quinn agreed, taking what seemed to be a steeling breath that got him to his feet.

Clairy stood, too, and walked along in her bare feet as he went to the porch steps. "Thanks for taking out all the trash," she said.

"No problem," Quinn assured her, catching sight of her still-curious neighbor.

She had the sense that Quinn was fighting the urge to kiss her again when he cast another glance in the neighbor's direction, but he didn't do it, much to Clairy's disappointment.

"Text me in the morning when you're ready for me to come over," he said, then reached a hand to her upper arm and squeezed it meaningfully.

"Good night," she whispered with as much voice as she could muster when just the feel of his big warm hand on her arm was tempting her to ignore the nosy neighbor and initiate another kiss anyway.

Or take Quinn inside after all…

But he let go of her and the option went down the porch steps with him.

"Night," he said with some of her disappointment ringing in his voice as he headed out to his truck.

Clairy stood there watching him until he was behind the wheel. He started the engine, then gave her one last wave that she returned.

Even after his truck disappeared down the street and her neighbor finally gave up his snooping to go in, Clairy stayed there on the porch as if it prolonged her time with Quinn for just a few seconds more.

And right then, she would have given just about anything if Quinn had driven around the block and come back.

Chapter Six

"If you don't want to hold Miss Poppy here, Quinn, then I'm taking her to sit on the porch—she loves it when we go outside and rock in the rocking chair, and I'm not passing up the chance to have a minute with my great-grandbaby."

Quinn held up both hands, palms out in surrender. "Have at it, Pops. I'm liable to break something that small."

"Coward," Tanner joked.

"Not denying it," Quinn answered with a laugh. "But I don't have to be insta-dad—you do."

"Yeah, you learn fast when you have to," Tanner said as they both watched Ben leave the kitchen with the three-month-old.

Tanner and Quinn were sitting at the table having coffee at 10:00 a.m. on Thursday morning. Tanner had shown up just to visit. His fiancée, Addie Markham, was having a spa day, and he had the baby on his own.

"So you're settling in to being a civilian just like that?" Quinn asked when they were alone.

"Yeah. Hard to believe, isn't it?" Tanner answered.

"It is," Quinn confirmed emphatically. "I mean, we knew Micah always had a time limit on his service. He wasn't going to be a lifer—he was going to stay in as long as it felt right to him, then resign so he could open his brewery. But you, me and Dalton…"

Tanner shrugged. "The road just forked."

"And you took the other route," Quinn confirmed for him.

But was it as simple as Tanner made it sound? "Did you take the other route happily?" he inquired then.

"Shocks me, too," Tanner said, as if he knew what Quinn was thinking. "But, yeah, I took it happily. Willingly. Eagerly. In fact, it was all my idea. Addie is…everything. I wake up every morning and can't believe my luck. And Poppy is mine—once that sank in, it took the blink of an eye for me to know that there was no way I could pack up and leave her behind for months at a time. No way I could miss even a day with her or being around to raise her, protect her. I just knew that not only was that what I had to do from now on, it was what I *wanted* to do. So my papers are in, I'm talking to a security company under government contract about a job I can do mainly from here, and what can I say? I'm buying civvies that you can borrow when you come to town—like you did last night."

"But I just saw you in Camp Lejeune *five* months ago, after Mac's death," Quinn commented, voicing more of his astonishment over the speed with which his brother had made such a huge decision. "Five months ago you were planning to go the distance, just like me, just like Mac."

"And if you had told me I'd be where I am now, telling you what I'm telling you, I would have said you were losing it," Tanner said, unflustered by Quinn's incredulity. Then he laughed and said, "Hell, that would have been the case even *one* month ago. For me, the marines were…I don't know…a calling, I guess. I thought I'd have that calling forever, stay in forever. Then I found out about Poppy, got to know Addie, and I started to hear a different call—"

"Out of obligation to them?" Quinn asked, trying to understand.

Tanner shook his head. "I'm not with Addie out of obligation. I'm with her because I want to be." He shrugged. "Something just happened. Something I didn't think would—or could—ever happen, and I wanted her more than I wanted to go on being a marine. I didn't want us to have a life where we're only together between missions or deployments or trainings or assignments. I wanted to be with her, with Poppy, day in, day out, through the good and the bad."

"I'm just having trouble picturing you like this," Quinn confessed.

"Maybe that's because for guys like you, and Mac, the marines are even more than a calling—they're in your blood, they go bone-deep. Mac died with his boots on. I'm sure you will, too."

Mention of Mac, of Mac's death, sobered Quinn considerably. Not only did it bring up the guilt he felt over his mentor's death, but Jill, the JAG attorney, had called just before Tanner's arrival this morning to tell him the results of her preliminary investigation and that the list of women with complaints about Mac was growing.

"Mac and I did see the marines mostly in the same way…mostly…" Quinn said, more to himself than to his brother, suffering all the heaviness brought on since his final visit with the General.

"Mostly?" Tanner caught that qualification and laughed again. "Since when?"

Quinn didn't answer. Instead, he said, "Tell me truthfully what you thought of Mac."

That turned Tanner's humor into a confused frown. "You know what I thought of him—he was a great man. A great marine."

"You and Mac crossed paths a time or two… What did you see from him?" Quinn persisted.

Tanner's frown deepened. "Are you kidding with this? I saw the toughest bastard in the corps. You know Micah and Dalton and I thought you were a glutton for punishment to go after him to whip you into shape when we were kids—experiencing it for myself when the time came made me *know* you were a glutton for punishment!"

"Living up to his standards, meeting his expectations, made you better, though, right?"

"Or else," Tanner said with another laugh, this one a pained comment on what had been required to meet the General's criteria.

"And that was true of everyone he commanded? Did you ever see him be harder on one person than another?"

"I did," Tanner admitted. "I was in a training with him about three years ago and he didn't think one of my guys was up to par. Mac rode him until he was. I almost felt sorry for the guy, but Mac did make him up his game, and believe me, we were grateful for it a couple of missions down the road." Tanner narrowed his eyes at Quinn. "Why? Was Mac losing it at the end? Getting soft?"

Quinn shook his head without hesitation. "Oh, no, not Mac."

"Why the questions, then? You want to make sure he lived up to his reputation right to his last breath?"

"Saw that for myself at Camp Lejeune," Quinn answered. He paused a moment, but felt compelled to press the matter, so he asked, "You ever think he went overboard? Hear secondhand that he had?"

It took Tanner a moment before he answered that question. "I don't know…" he said. "He demanded more than anybody I've ever known. I heard plenty of complaints about him, but I can't say it was from anyone I ever wanted to have to rely on. And you know what it's like in the trenches—you don't want to be there with somebody who *couldn't* pass muster with Mac when your life depends on it."

"So no matter how rough Mac was on anybody, you would have rather had him weed them out than not? Even if he went against protocol, regulations?"

"Protocol and regulations? Wasn't Mac about as by-the-book as it was humanly possible to be?"

"What if he wasn't? What if he thought it wasn't for the greater good to be strictly by-the-book when the book got changed?"

Tanner was staring at him, frowning, obviously puzzled by what Quinn was pressing him for.

Then Tanner said, "I don't know. I'm not even sure what you're getting at. I do know that I've butted up against new regs, new protocols here and there. Not a lot, but…" He shrugged. "I've had occasions. It isn't always easy to just swallow changes."

Quinn nodded his agreement. "Yeah, I've been there, too. But…" But what? Quinn asked himself, unsure where he was going as he struggled to wade through what his last visit with his mentor had left him with.

Rather than find a way to finish this line of inquiry, he turned more philosophical and said, "You think we ever know everything there is to know about anyone?"

"Will there ever be anyone who you let know everything there is to know about you?" Tanner asked without skipping a beat.

"Spoken like somebody who's seen and done some hard things himself. Things he'll never be open about," Quinn said with an entirely humorless chuckle.

"Spoken *to* somebody who's seen and done some hard things *him*self," Tanner countered.

"For the greater good," Quinn added, repeating his own earlier words.

"So will I ever want—or let—every bit of me to be known?" Tanner said. "No. And so also, no—no one will ever know everything there is to know about me."

Quinn conceded that point with arched eyebrows, then focused his eyes on his coffee mug.

"But it seems like something pretty big is weighing on you…" Tanner commented. "We can keep it just between us if you need to get it off your chest."

Quinn shook his head. "Thanks, but…not yet…" It was all going to come out, but he thought Mac's family needed to be the first to know. "I have to pack up a ton of Mac's stuff to get to Clairy today—"

Tanner laughed yet again, this time the laugh of a prodding brother as the tone between them took another switch. "And the voice gets softer when you say her name."

"Oh, yeah, right," Quinn said, spurning the suggestion of what Tanner was implying.

Tanner narrowed his eyes at Quinn. "Are you getting some comeuppance for how you treated her all those years ago? Maybe you're a little sweet on somebody who could pay you back hard?"

"Hey, you may have been bitten by some kind of fierce lovebug, but don't put that off on me," Quinn warned.

"Wouldn't think of it. I'm sure you're above that."

"Yep."

"Even with a little redheaded beauty who could give you a run for your money," Tanner said sarcastically.

"Yep," Quinn agreed again, as if that statement was so true it didn't deserve to get a rise out of him.

Their grandfather came in from the front porch then, bringing an early warning of the reason for it.

"Uh, Dad, hope you brought a diaper," Ben said to Tanner as he approached the kitchen.

"And that's my cue to get to work loading Mac's stuff," Quinn said. He stood and took his cup to the dishwasher, then hightailed it out the back door and to the shed.

His grandfather used the shed as a workroom, but

when Quinn had shipped the packing boxes filled with the General's things home, Ben had stored them in one corner of the shed to await Quinn's arrival. That was where Quinn found them now.

There were more than he remembered—too many to carry to the front of the house, where his truck was parked. So he left the shed to bring his truck as far around back and close to the shed as he could get it.

Discussing the General had allowed Quinn one of the few breaks from incessantly thinking about Clairy, but just the mention of her moments before put her back in his thoughts as he moved his truck.

It wasn't Clairy alone on his mind, though. It was also the fact that beginning that afternoon they'd be going through her father's things together, revisiting the General's entire career, his history, his decisions and actions. And it was coming after Jill's call this morning.

I'm going to have to tell you. The whole damn story...

Those early weeks after Mac's death, he'd wrestled with his own guilt over their argument possibly causing it and with keeping his mouth shut to protect Mac's memory. Then he'd decided he couldn't do that for the sake of the women marines, but he still hadn't considered airing that last fight and the potential consequences of it. But now...

Now that something was going on between him and Clairy on a personal level and he was going to have to tell her about her father, tell her that he didn't know what the outcome of a formal inquiry into Mac's actions would be, now that he was going to have to confess that he and Mac had battled, it was going to come out that that battle might have been what led to her father's death.

And now that Clairy was uppermost in every thought in his head, what was that going to mean?

Are you going to start hating me all over again?

That thought was particularly hard for Quinn to have because he didn't think it would take much to cause her to start hating him again.

And while at the start of this he'd only been interested in coming to a peace accord with Clairy to get through this memorial-and-museum work with as little fuss as possible, somehow her not hating him had become important to him.

Really important.

"But today's the day..." he told himself sternly, worrying about just how important Clairy not hating him had become.

Maybe just how important Clairy had become to him...

"That's some risky business," he warned himself on the heels of that thought, which had slipped in on its own. "You know you're not ready to get involved with anyone," he reminded himself out loud, as if it might carry more weight if he heard it rather than merely thought it. "You've blown it bad with

two women already—worse than bad with Laine—
and you don't have any business messing around
with someone else until you figure out how much of
Mac's disregard for any woman's feelings you might
have channeled."

But ready or not…

Quinn sighed as he slid another box into the bed
of his truck.

What was churning around inside of him when
it came to Clairy shouldn't be. But Tanner's crack
about him being sweet on her wasn't wrong. He
didn't know if he'd fooled his brother or not, but to
say that he was *sweet* on Clairy was actually way
too mild a description. That kiss last night had been
more hot and spicy than sweet.

Jeez, what a kiss…

A kiss he shouldn't have let go as far as it had—
something he was reminded of, especially when telling her about her father nagged at him.

Nagged at him and brought up the questions he'd
been chewing on for a while now about himself and
where he went going forward with his own relationships. What he really wanted.

Looking at his own history with women through
the same lens he was now looking at his mentor,
he'd come to realize that he couldn't keep getting
involved with women in the same way he had been.
It had become a pattern with him. Not consciously,
not intentionally—he hadn't even recognized it until

he'd begun to compare himself to Mac—but a pattern of general disregard for what was important to a woman involved with him, a general disregard for their own wants and needs. A pattern of treating them as if they weren't as important as he was, as the marines were. And it had to stop.

It had to stop, he had to regroup and he had to decide how to proceed from here. He had to figure out if he should accept that serving his country in the marines was the be-all and end-all for him forever—what he'd believed since he was a child.

If it was, then from now on he had to make sure the only women he spent any time with were women who were satisfied being relegated to recreational status. Or women who could accept never being as important to him as the marines, but were still willing to have a future with him being fully aware of that…if women like that existed.

But one way or another, until he actually figured it out, he shouldn't be messing around with any woman, let alone with Clairy.

He just couldn't seem to help himself…

But you need to!

As long as he had as much weighing on him as he did, until he sorted out everything he needed to sort out about Mac, about how much his mentor might have colored his own views and actions, he needed to keep to the straight and narrow.

And that went double—triple—with Clairy.

He was just losing confidence in his ability to stick to that straight and narrow when it came to her.

"But telling her what you have to tell her now might take it out of your hands..."

"It's up to you, honey, but I think it should be known that even big important generals start out as little boys."

"You know we would have to fight him to put it in, though—he *never* would have let us do it willingly," Clairy laughingly answered her grandmother.

Clairy had put off Quinn this morning because it was the only time in Mim's busy new schedule for her to come over to go through family photos. Clairy's goal was to find out what her grandmother might want contributed to the General's memorial.

The elderly woman had made several choices that documented the early high points and transitional moments of her son's life—graduations, awards, being carried on the shoulders of teammates after football victories, becoming school president.

But on a lighter, sweeter side, she'd also come across a picture of Mac when he was four years old. In the weathered black-and-white snapshot he was wearing his father's army jacket and cap—the jacket hung to the floor, while the cap was tipped back on the small boy's head to rest on his shoulders. And her dad was giving a touching salute.

It was a cute picture, and because it represented a

branch of the service, Mim thought it should be the start of the display, to show the General's early, innocent interest in the military.

Clairy liked the idea but still felt inclined to point out that her father would have considered it undignified. That was what she was doing as they walked out to Mim's car after the lunch Clairy had made for them.

"Well, now he doesn't have a say," Mim insisted. "And I'm his mother and I want one picture of him as my little boy."

"Okay," Clairy conceded. "I'll have it framed with a plaque underneath it saying it was donated by you."

"Good."

Mim opened her car door, gave Clairy a hug and said, "I better get going. Harry is waiting."

"Tell him I said hello," Clairy instructed as her grandmother started the engine and pulled away from the curb at a snail's pace.

Then she hurried back inside with barely an hour to get ready for Quinn's scheduled arrival at three.

She'd showered early and now dressed in a pair of black ankle-length slacks and a pale blue sleeveless cotton shirt with a ruffled front edge that crossed over to close with four buttons that ran from her hip to her waist to form a modest V neckline. As the time neared, she bent over, swooshing her hair to hang free so she could brush it from underneath. Then she put the long, full mass into a high ponytail with a scarf tied around it. She added soft pink lip gloss and a pair of slip-on sandals for the final touches, then went downstairs and stopped near the living room's picture window just as Quinn drove up.

He parked his big white truck where her grandmother's sedan had been, and that was all it took for Clairy to forget what she'd been about to do and stop where she was as he turned off the engine and got out.

Was her heart actually racing?

Just because of him?

Come on, Clairy, get it together!

But her heart *was* racing and it just went on racing as she watched him come up the walkway.

Gone were the slacks and shirt of the previous evening. He'd replaced them with tan cargo pants and a navy blue crewneck T-shirt with the marine emblem over his left, well-accentuated pec.

Back to rugged, Clairy thought as she watched him approach the house, wishing she could find fault with the well-groomed stubble, the artfully disarrayed hair and the more casual clothes.

But she failed miserably.

So miserably that for a split second she fantasized about skipping what they had planned today, so she could drag him inside, close the door behind him and spend the afternoon making out with him on the couch like a couple of teenagers...

Shaking off that idea, she retraced her steps to

hold open the screen door for him. "Hi. Come in," she invited.

"How you doin'?" he greeted her as he entered, both of them sounding like they were barely acquainted.

"I'm ready to dig in to my father's storied career to see what we're dealing with," she answered, having needed to bolster herself a little in anticipation of wading through the evidence of all the things her father had prioritized over her.

She had no idea why that brought a frown to that handsome face, and it wasn't explained as Quinn came in and said only, "So, to the attic?"

He definitely didn't sound eager. But it occurred to her that while she was facing the evidence of all she'd failed to compete with in her father's career, Quinn was facing reminders of things he'd shared with the General.

They were both revisiting their separate griefs, and she realized she shouldn't expect the job ahead to be lighthearted, the way going through pictures of happy family times with Mim had been.

"I brought down everything I found in the attic," Clairy informed Quinn. "But since my father gave you instructions for where to find things, you better check it out and make sure I didn't miss anything."

"Sure."

And weren't they just so down-to-business, as if

barely more than twelve hours ago they hadn't been locked together at the lips.

But getting down to business was as it should be, Clairy told herself.

Even if last night had ended the way it had.

In the attic, Quinn found only one box of her father's things that Clairy had missed. As they added her boxes to those in the back of his truck, he explained that his boxes contained things Mac had given him since putting the plan for the memorial and library in the works, as well as the contents of Mac's Camp Lejeune office and private quarters.

"I guess it was lucky you were there to pack all his things when he died," Clairy commented along the way.

That produced another dark frown and no response from Quinn.

Which was essentially the tone of the day and evening as they worked. Quinn was unusually quiet, solemn and somber.

Clairy continued to attribute it to grief—something she felt more strongly herself as they went through her father's things. Underneath her resentments and longings and regrets, the General had still been her father and she'd loved him despite it all. If she hadn't, she wouldn't have cared that she hadn't seemed important to him. And as she and Quinn went through Mac's things, it was her own grief at the forefront, too.

Late in the afternoon, they were interrupted by

the delivery of the display cases she'd ordered for the memorial and the sofa designated for her office on the second floor.

Clairy tried to persuade the deliverymen to bring everything to their final destinations, but they refused, leaving it all just inside the library's front entrance.

"I'll bring my dolly and we'll do that tomorrow," Quinn promised.

Clairy had wondered if today would be the end of their work together—after all, once he made the decisions about what was to be included in the memorial and how he wanted it presented, it was just up to Clairy to carry out his instructions. Hearing him promise more of his time and physical prowess went a long way in brightening her mood as they returned to the job at hand.

For dinner they ordered pizza at eight, eating as they did a tour of everything they'd spent the previous hours setting out on the large library tables.

Because her father's final wishes were for Quinn to have the last word on what would best memorialize him, Clairy took notes on Quinn's decisions on what should be displayed, where, how and in what order.

She lobbied for a few changes, and when she did, Quinn accepted her suggestions, but on the whole, the memorial was more Quinn's vision than hers. Clairy reasoned that not only was that how the General had wanted it, but Quinn had also known and understood her father, what he wanted and how he thought better than she had.

They finished about nine o'clock and it was a relief to Clairy to have made it through the emotions this dive into her father's things brought with it. She felt as if a weight had been lifted from her shoulders.

But it didn't seem as if the same could be said of Quinn. In fact, he seemed so distracted by his own thoughts that twice when Clairy asked him something she'd had to repeat herself because he didn't hear her the first time. And more than the somber expression he'd carried throughout their hours of discussing her father, he appeared to sink even further into brooding.

Even so, rather than ending the evening when they reached a stopping point with the memorial, he measured her newly arrived sofa, the opening and inside of the elevator, and said, "I think between the two of us we could get this upstairs to your office tonight."

"Today hasn't done you in?" Clairy ventured, uncertain what was going on with him, but worrying that he might just want away from memories of her father, and maybe of her, too.

"I think I can push myself," he said facetiously.

"I'm willing," she said, flinching internally at the unintentional innuendo that hovered around the edges of that comment.

But Quinn was still so mired in whatever was on

his mind that he didn't even catch it. He just went to the tufted leather sofa so they could slide it to the elevator.

When they got it there, they upended it to get it in. Then, since Clairy alone could fit in the elevator with it, she stood alongside to steady it for the ride and Quinn met her on the second floor.

They slid it to her office, where they put it against the wall she'd designated for it.

Quinn pulled off the protective plastic and sat in the center to give it a test-drive.

"That's a lot more comfortable than it looks," he proclaimed. He patted the seat. "Try it out."

Clairy did. "It isn't bad," she said, judging for herself. "I chose it because it looked stately, something for a library or den. But when you order online, you never know how it is to sit on it. It could have gone either way."

"But this is comfortable enough to sleep on if you ever get stuck here overnight."

"I can't imagine why that would happen, but it feels pretty good now—it's been a long day."

But she didn't want Quinn to take the comment as a cue to call it a night, because she wasn't ready for that. Even if he was quiet, preoccupied company. She at least wanted the chance to draw him out of his melancholy.

So before he could use her words against her, she pivoted enough for her spine to meet the couch's corner, where the sofa's back became the sofa's arm without a change in height. Facing him, she made a guess... "Today was hard for you—going through my father's things, everything being a reminder of him."

"For you, too, wasn't it?"

"Yes..." she answered, hedging. "But it was a reminder for me of where he really lived his life, what his life really was to him and how I was a distant afterthought in it, not a part of it. For you it had to be a reminder of what the two of you have always been about, what the two of you have shared since you were an eight-year-old kid, that you don't have him to share it with anymore."

Quinn turned enough to face her, too, laying his arm along the back edge of the couch, but he still didn't respond readily. And when he did, there was some hedging in his voice, too.

"Yeah, all of that... But there's more now...more even just today."

She wasn't sure exactly what that meant. "Grief?"

"Sure..."

"But something else, too?" Clairy persisted. She recalled what he'd said on Sunday night over dinner in the square after she'd given him the first tour of the library. "Is this what you said before about knowing something now that you hadn't known before?" she asked, her curiosity about that revived.

Once more he was slow to reply, and even when

he did, he didn't give her a straight answer. "It's been a rough five months, Clairy. But there's some things I have to tell you."

He stalled, looked at the floor, obviously reluctant. Then he looked squarely at her and sighed. "You're not going to thank me for the information," he warned.

Clairy's concerns were mounting, but she hid them. "I don't know what could be such a big deal— my father was about the straightest arrow who ever lived. Unless he had some kind of secret life…"

"No secret life. But something he convinced himself threatened the foundation of the United States Marine Corps—something he was willing to bend, or break, the rules over."

"Robert 'Mac' McKinnon a rule-breaker?" Clairy laughed, albeit nervously. "Come on…"

"I never knew it of him before. But when he chose to, he did it the way he did everything—in the extreme."

Stress was making Clairy impatient. "Okay. So if you're going to tell me, tell me."

Quinn closed his eyes, arched his eyebrows and took another moment to gather himself.

After a deep breath, he said, "I think you know how Mac felt about women in the military—"

"He *hated* it with a passion. He said there was nothing a man couldn't do and in the military that's how it should be. Women were just a distraction.

The one time I said I wanted to join—hoping that would make him like me as well as he liked you—he blew up!"

"I remember," Quinn confirmed. "His 'no women in the military' was a pretty regular Mac rant."

"Mac rant," Clairy repeated. "That's a good name for them. He had an opinion on everything. He never thought he was wrong, no one could convince him that he was, and he liked to hammer his point home over and over again," Clairy said.

"That's what I called a Mac rant," Quinn confirmed affectionately, as if that aspect of the General's personality had amused him. His fondness for her father was still clearly in play under the surface of this.

Whatever *this* was…

Quinn sobered again. "But when push came to shove—when regulations and protocols changed, progressed—he might have bitched, but he did what we all do. He followed orders, made the changes. Mac was old-school—"

"*Old* old-school when it came to this."

"But I never knew him not to do the right thing. So when it came to women in the marines, in combat, regardless of his opinions and gripes, when that started happening, I thought he was doing what he was supposed to do."

"You *thought* he was, but he wasn't?"

"We talked about women in the marines more times than I can count. The marines are—"

"*The toughest of the tough*—I know," Clairy said, repeating what she'd heard both her father and Quinn say.

Quinn didn't comment on that; he merely went on. "We agreed that exceptions shouldn't be given for women in the marines. We agreed that they needed to meet the same standards every marine needs to meet, that if they couldn't, they shouldn't be marines. We agreed that to be in the field with women, on a mission with women, we all had to be able to rely on them the same way we rely on any other marine."

"In other words, there were parts of what my father was against that you supported."

"Parts. Where we disagreed was that women *could* meet the standards, do the job—Mac thought that women were always a weak link. But I'd seen women who were good, capable marines and I told Mac so. I said that if they proved themselves the same way men did, they had a right to do the same jobs."

Quinn got points with her for that, even if it did surprise her that he not only held that viewpoint, but had also grown into someone who could— and would—disagree with the bullheaded Mac McKinnon. "But, of course, that didn't budge my father from his opinion because nothing and no one ever did."

"No, it didn't change his mind," Quinn confirmed. "But he had me convinced that it was all just academic—that while it might be begrudging and reluctant, while he'd likely never put a woman in a crucial position himself, he was still following guidelines, protocols, laws and regulations about female personnel."

"Only he wasn't?"

Quinn didn't seem eager to admit that. And didn't at first. "The only thing my side of the argument accomplished was to make him hide what he was doing from me. Until I showed up earlier than expected at Camp Lejeune five months ago and overheard him giving orders to someone who didn't dare buck him, someone who was trying to reason with him, who was pointing out the glaring difference—the risks, and that safety measures were being removed—in what he was setting up for the two women trainees."

"He was making it *riskier* and purposely less safe for the women than the men?"

"Mac always set the bar higher for us all, which sometimes added some risk, but it was worth it— it made us better, stronger. But this was more than that. Worse… After I heard what I heard, I asked him what the hell he was doing. It was pretty clear that I wasn't supposed to have heard. He got more defensive than I'd ever seen him. He just went off—"

"It never took much to get a rise out of him," Clairy said, familiar with her father's tirades.

"He said it was bad enough to have women marines at all, but women in special ops? They especially didn't belong there and he wasn't standing for it. He admitted to me that he was going to make them fail, come hell or high water. And once he got started on his rant, he said some things that made me think this wasn't new or just about women in special ops…"

Quinn paused, clearly not relishing speaking against his mentor. Clairy had the impression that he saw this as a betrayal.

But he seemed to push himself to do it anyway, as if he was convinced he had to. "At Camp Lejeune, the orders Mac gave would have put the two women trainees in genuine jeopardy. They were strong, exemplary marines—they'd weathered everything he'd thrown at them. So he was stacking the deck against them, and that upped the odds that they might not have come out in one piece." Quinn's disbelief that the General would do something like that echoed in his voice.

Clairy understood how difficult it had to have been for him to discover that the man he'd idolized—the man he'd fashioned himself after—had flaws. But her father having flaws was not news to her, and while it wasn't easy to learn what she was learning about the General, it didn't hit her the way it did Quinn.

Still, she wanted to make sure she understood completely. "And my father knew that he was putting the women in higher danger?"

"He knew," Quinn said, as if he wished it had been

otherwise. "He knew exactly what he was doing—he said it was what he had to do."

There was a note in Quinn's voice that must have been similar to the tone her father had used, because he made it sound reasonable.

Then it was Quinn's own conscience that finished what he'd been about to say. "But this was bad, Clairy…"

Another pause, another moment when Clairy thought Quinn was struggling with his loyalty to her father. She could see how torn he was between that and doing what he thought was right.

But eventually he continued. "I thought about the other things Mac had said—they made me wonder how long he'd been at this, how far he might have already gone with women assigned to him for combat. I decided I'd better do some digging, beginning with Camp Lejeune, where I made sure the specially designed training they'd been assigned was postponed. It wasn't easy to get people to talk honestly to me, because my connection to Mac made me the last person anyone wanted to squeal to—"

"That can't surprise you," Clairy said.

"I always did have his back…" Quinn responded, as if now he wasn't so sure that had been wise. "But it wasn't only that there was suspicion that I might be testing them on behalf of Mac. I talked to one former officer who had served in a unit I'd also served in under Mac, and found out that part of Tom's orders to make life harder for any woman in the unit was to also make sure I was kept completely in the dark about it—"

"So there were times when this was being done right under your nose?"

"I guess so," he admitted reluctantly. "And that made me analyze things that I'd seen myself, incidents I'd written off, justified with my own opinion that if any woman couldn't cut it, they didn't belong with us…"

There was more hesitation, more reluctance to talk.

Then Quinn again seemed to force himself.

"In retrospect, I realized that I *had* seen a few things where Mac could have been purposely putting a woman in harm's way. I remembered even questioning him about his orders once or twice, but he'd said he was giving the woman the chance to prove herself to the men, to gain their respect. I remembered thinking at the time that had validity, that whenever I was assigned a woman—while I never put them in any position that could get them killed—I did use them sparingly, hold them back until I was convinced they really could cut it, so—"

"You'd bought it."

"And I shouldn't have," he said flatly. "Looking at those times through a new lens, I started to see that Mac was setting those women up to fail, hoping to show them and everyone else that they *couldn't* do it, to scare them off. I think that if they were hurt in the process, getting them sent home or transferred out of combat duty—or at least reassigned so he didn't have to deal with them—was worth it to him."

As all of this was beginning to sink in, Clairy realized that she was less stunned by her father's willingness to take some kind of action to get women out of the marines than Quinn was. In fact, she saw an added element to it that meant something else to her.

She'd had so many years of feeling as if, to her father, she mattered less than Quinn, that she was invisible, insignificant, irrelevant. So many years when she'd felt as if her father hadn't liked her, as if she'd somehow disappointed him, as if she wasn't enough, as if there was something wrong with her.

But to hear now that he'd felt this strongly even against women striving for what his entire life had been about opened her eyes to a facet of the General that she'd never considered. And that caused her to wonder if maybe her father had been so much of a sexist that he'd seen not just her, but *all* women as having less worth than men, that in his eyes *no* woman could rise to his standards or be worthy of anything but insignificant status.

And if that was true, it shed new light on her relationship with him.

Maybe it hadn't been about her…

Maybe it hadn't even been about Quinn commandeering her father's attention.

Maybe this was wholly her father's failure.

Quinn was lost in his own thoughts and didn't seem to notice that Clairy had been, too. But then he began again. "After just the quick-and-dirty look into it that I did, after what I opened my own eyes to, I had to put a stop to it," he said, his furrowed brow even more deeply troubled with that announcement. "We had one hell of a fight that night, Clairy..."

Why did that sound like a confession with a plea for understanding? For mercy, maybe?

"I told him I knew what he'd been doing, and I gave him an ultimatum—I told him he needed to step down and put in for retirement."

"But if he didn't?"

"I said that I'd formally report him."

That hung as heavily in the air as Clairy knew it had to have felt to Quinn when he'd made the threat.

"Would you have?" she asked quietly.

"Yes."

No hesitation, no wavering—only strength, determination and sorrow.

"What did he say?"

"One hell of a fight..." Quinn repeated. "We went back and forth until after one a.m. It was as ugly as it could have been. But ultimately, he knew I meant what I said, that I'd follow through..." Quinn smiled the saddest smile Clairy had ever seen. "He said he didn't doubt it because it was what he'd made of me..."

This pause was the longest of them all, with Quinn

looking past her. She had the sense that he was reliving that night, that fight.

"Then I left," he said ominously. "And when I came back at zero six hundred, I found his aide there..." Quinn looked Clairy in the eye again, as if he had to. "Mac had had the heart attack sometime between when I left and when I went back..."

Clairy stared at him as she began to absorb what he was telling her.

She'd known that Quinn was at Camp Lejeune visiting her father when he'd died. She'd known the heart attack had happened during the night, that he'd been alone at the time. She hadn't known that just shortly before that heart attack her father had had a heated confrontation and been given a career-ending ultimatum by the man he'd considered his son.

She wasn't sure what to think, what to feel.

But as that information hit her and she analyzed her own response, she discovered that it was sympathy for Quinn and what it had to mean to him that was uppermost in her mind.

"You feel like you caused the heart attack," she commented in a near whisper.

"It was a bad fight, Clairy," he reiterated. "I was making him do something he wanted *never* to do—leave the marines."

And Quinn's remorse was so huge it was almost palpable in the air.

"There was one thing you *didn't* know about him,"

Clairy said. "One thing that didn't make his heart attack a surprise to Mim and me because we were the only people—outside of his doctors—who knew it. He wasn't well, Quinn."

Quinn's brow furrowed even more. "What do you mean he wasn't well?"

"A year ago he came to Denver without warning. He said he hadn't been feeling well and he wanted to see a private doctor, that he was going to pay for it out of his own pocket so it was completely off the record. He said he didn't want any decline in his health known by anyone in the marines because he wasn't going to be forced into a medical discharge."

"That sounds like Mac. But he didn't even tell me?"

Clairy heard in Quinn's voice what had been in her own so many times—the shock and disbelief at learning that the General had excluded him. So she understood what had to be going through Quinn's mind. "He knew you well enough to keep what he was doing to women marines from you—he probably knew you were by-the-book enough not to let him go on working when he shouldn't have."

Quinn's only response was another raise of his eyebrows that confirmed her theory.

"Anyway," Clairy said, to get to the point, "when I took him for his appointment, the internist sent him from his office straight to the emergency room. A cardiologist there did a full workup—his heart was in bad, bad shape. The cardiologist didn't know how he was still walking around. Apparently, he'd already had a heart attack—"

"Something he'd felt? Or some kind of silent thing?"

"He knew it. It's what brought him to Denver— apparently, he'd had a physical the January before, gotten a clean bill of health. But in late May he'd been alone, had chest pain and passed out. He was still alone when he came to, he didn't feel well, but—" Clairy shrugged "—you know how he was. He wasn't going to let it keep him down. Still, he figured whatever it had been hadn't been good. That's when he decided he was only going to see a civilian doctor—"

"And went to Denver," Quinn said.

"The cardiologist called in a surgeon—they wanted to schedule him for immediate valve replacement surgery and a pacemaker. The cardiologist said Mac needed to retire, change his diet and lifestyle, that he'd need to take medications to thin his blood, and a half-dozen other drugs if he had any hope of his heart not giving out at any moment—"

"And he wouldn't do it," Quinn said, making an educated guess.

"He wouldn't even consider it," Clairy confirmed. "Mim and I both went round and round with him, and in spite of the cardiologist telling him point-blank that he was asking for a massive heart attack that could come at any time, he said he'd rather go out that way than live twenty more years not being a marine. The most he would agree to do was take the training command at Camp Lejeune rather than more active duty—"

"So *that's* why he did that! I wondered but he wouldn't give me a straight answer when I asked him."

"He was a ticking time bomb," Clairy said, finishing what she'd been about to say.

"And I threatened him with losing what he would have rather died than give up..."

Clairy had meant to decrease Quinn's feelings of guilt, not increase them. "My point is—the blame was his own, Quinn," she said more firmly, in hopes of convincing him he wasn't at fault. "The only thing that mattered to my father was to do things his own way and, in this, that meant to be a marine right to the end—"

"Which was what he was fighting for with me."

"You offered him the option of just stepping down gracefully before what he was doing was exposed— which it probably would have been, because eventually someone would have blown the whistle—and he refused. The heart doctor offered him help and he refused. Nobody could protect him from himself," Clairy concluded.

Quinn shook his head, and Clairy had the impression that nothing she said was causing him to relinquish what he clearly saw as his part in his mentor's death. "It still shouldn't have been me, of all people, who—"

Clairy decided to take a different approach. "I understand how you see this," she said. "But it had to be you who went up against him over the women he was putting in jeopardy. No one else—*no one*—carried the weight with him that you did. No one meant as much to him as you did. So no one else could have stopped him. And if you hadn't, if you had let him go on doing what he was doing even after you knew, then any injury any woman suffered at his hands *would* have been as much your fault as his."

Quinn conceded to that only with another raise of his eyebrows, which compelled Clairy to go on trying to lessen the weight he was carrying about this.

"You told me yourself when we talked about Brad, about the way you were raised, about your mother pushing you not to let anything stand in your way when you wanted something, that you've learned that even as a marine that can't always come into play. I'm thinking that when you said you just saw that same philosophy in someone else gone really wrong, you were talking about what my father was doing…"

Clairy paused for Quinn to confirm. She got only a slow nod.

"And it was the marines—my father—who taught you how to temper that, how to use your powers only for good," she said with the same attempt to lighten the conversation that he had when he'd originally used the turn of phrase.

"That's what you did," she went on. "Difficult as

it was to do with one of the people most important to you. But the bottom line, Quinn, is that you were doing the right thing. My father wasn't. His health, accepting the risks that came with not treating it, was separate. And the fact that that was when his heart gave out wasn't on you—it honestly could have happened even if the two of you had just spent the best night of his life."

Quinn smiled another small, sad smile that didn't tell her whether or not she'd convinced him.

When he didn't say anything one way or another to let her know, she decided he might need to gain some more perspective on his own now that he had the full picture.

Whether or not that was true, he went on. "And there's more," he said ominously, his bushy eyebrows heading for his hairline once more. "For a while after he died, I considered keeping what I'd learned to myself to protect Mac's reputation. But the longer I sat on it…the more wrong I saw in not looking at it from the perspective of the women. I put in a call to a JAG lawyer I know and told her…"

"So ultimately you did report him," Clairy marveled.

"I'm sorry, Clairy—"

"No! It's what you should have done! I just can't believe that you—of all people—did it!"

"I wanted to protect him…to protect his memory," Quinn lamented. "But not only did the women he might have done harm to have a right to…I don't know…some kind of justice or—like you said—to be heard, but I don't know who else might have willingly gone along with Mac, who might still be doing what Mac was doing, and I just couldn't let it go without…blowing the whistle, I guess…" Though he clearly didn't like to label himself as a whistleblower.

"My friend Jill has been looking into it," Quinn continued. "I trusted that she wouldn't open a can of worms that didn't need opening if what Mac had done was on a smaller scale than it seemed to me—"

"What you were hoping was the case," Clairy guessed.

"More than you can ever know."

"But it wasn't on a small enough scale to be inconsequential."

Quinn shook his head. "Jill called me this morning. She's found enough to open an investigation by an independent committee. Not only into Mac—it looks like he had some cohorts doing this kind of thing, too, so I guess the best I can tell you is that Mac won't be the only one whose name and reputation will take a hit for this…"

"But there will be a hit," Clairy surmised.

"I'm sorry." Quinn's tone said he was sorry for so many things. "And when it comes to the memorial… I guess it's up to you to decide what you'll do with it… It could change the way he's remembered…cast a dishonorable shadow…or you could ignore it… I don't know…"

Clairy thought about what to do, thought about the man her father had been, his accomplishments, his flaws, her own complaints with him. "He was a long way from perfect," she said.

"And this could give you a platform to air that," he said with some trepidation, still in many ways following what seemed to be an instinct to be the guardian of Mac's memory. "Just please don't forget that even though Mac screwed up at the end he was still a great marine," Quinn seemed compelled to add.

Clairy thought about it all.

Clairy did keep that in mind as she considered how to handle all this new information. Did she want to air her own personal grievances with her father in public? Would that serve any purpose or make anything better?

She couldn't see how.

Instead, it seemed to cast her as a victim and she didn't want that role. She preferred to leave the way her father had treated her as a portion of her own history, something that had contributed to who she was, a lesson she'd learned in the kind of parent she *didn't* want to be, and the kind of father she wouldn't want to give her own children.

But what about the rest? Where *did* Mac's actions against women fit into the memorial to Mac?

She didn't think it could—or should—be overlooked. That didn't seem fair or just to the women marines.

After pondering it, Clairy said, "I think it will have to be noted somehow," she concluded. "I'll have to figure out how to present it—"

"Don't forget that there *are* women marines who made it in spite of Mac's best efforts, and they see that as a testament to their strength and stamina and resiliency in the face of the worst that could be dished out to them. I get that the women who suffered and failed should have a voice, but you have to give credit where credit is due to the ones who likely suffered and still succeeded."

"I'll try to relay the facts and include that. I'll give the reasoning behind what he did and point out that it's outdated thinking rightfully having a light shone on it. I can get hold of any photographs of only women marines and I can display them above the text and the outcome of the investigation," Clairy proposed. "Hopefully I'll be able to say that the good that came out of it—assuming good will come out of it—is that this kind of thing will stop?"

"I like that. It turns a negative into a positive. Even if the negative is on Mac, I don't think it undermines the good he did. It just shows that he had flaws…"

Flaws that Clairy thought Quinn was slowly coming to admit Mac had. To accept that Mac had.

"There was nothing warm or fuzzy about my

father at any time, in any way. That's what made him who he was, and this will be another facet of it."

Quinn nodded. "I can live with that."

"It goes a long way that you've set the wheels into motion to stop it, though, to give a voice to the women he mistreated. Do you want to be given the credit?"

"No, leave me out of it. I'm sorry it had to be done—this kind of thing shouldn't be going on," Quinn said quietly. "But there's no way I want credit for something that puts a smear on Mac."

Clairy understood that, understood how difficult this had to have been for him, and she thought that what Quinn had done spoke volumes about him.

Obviously he didn't see that, but he did seem relieved as he looked at her with warmth in his eyes. "Thanks for not letting this last misstep of Mac's overshadow everything else about him. It's more than he deserved from you after being the kind of father he was."

"I had you worried, though, didn't I?" she said, to give him a hard time.

But it didn't work, because his expression relaxed even more as he looked intently into her eyes. "Nah, I wasn't worried. What I'm learning every day is that there's a whole lot more to you than I ever knew or gave you credit for. And it's making me think that Mac really missed the boat by not seeing all there is to you."

Quinn didn't seem to be missing anything about her now, because he was studying her intently. And she liked that.

Maybe too much…

It had been a long afternoon and evening of work, topped off by a stressful conversation that had taken all the fight out of Clairy.

But she wasn't alone in that. Peering into Quinn's striking face, she saw that some of the marine in him had been stripped away to expose the man who had been carrying quite a burden for the last five months and needed a bit of a break himself now that he'd shared it.

And it was as if the sharing of it had brought them closer, had cultivated something new between them.

His arm was still propped on the top edge of the sofa's back. Then his hand rose up to one end of the scarf that held her hair in the high ponytail. A tug made the knot come free, and the long waves fell around her face and shoulders at the same time he moved closer to her.

"Yeah, this couch is kind of nice…" he said. "It's not a bad place to land after a rough day. To regroup…"

Were they just regrouping?

Or were they returning to what had ended the night before? Restarting it…?

Clairy wasn't opposed to restarting it. Not only had she wanted him to kiss her again since he'd stopped last night, but the previous hour's exchange had also left her craving solace, the comfort of arms around her.

His arms around her.

So much so that she wanted to encourage whatever he had in mind and brought her feet up under her hip to alter her own position and subtract another inch from the distance between them.

Answering an urge for contact, she laid her palm to the side of his oh-so-handsome face, drinking in the warmth of his skin as his blue, blue eyes delved into hers.

"Mac's daughter..." he whispered to himself.

Clairy wasn't sure whether he was marveling at that fact, reminding himself of it or warning himself to be cautious.

But whatever the meaning, it didn't stop him from drawing nearer as if something was pulling him. Pulling him into a kiss that was soft and sweet, that answered her need for comfort and seemed to have roots in that new bond between them.

But it wasn't long before comfort was found. And then what had been cut short the previous evening began again all on its own.

First lips parted and the kiss remained soft, seeking. Until his tongue came to say hello and hers greeted it joyously.

Quinn's arm came around her to pull her the rest of the way to him while his free hand combed through her hair to clasp the back of her head. He kissed her all the more deeply, their mouths open wider as restraint dropped away.

Clairy's hand drifted from his cheek to his shoulder as that fantasy she'd had of making out with him on the couch at home that afternoon became a reality.

A heady reality that brought her other hand to his T-shirted pec. The rock-solid feel of those muscles just fed her soul and she couldn't resist exploring them. His chest. His shoulders. His broad back. His biceps…

And with each exploration, she got a little more turned on. Then a little more. Then more still, until the idea of just kissing wasn't enough.

Her head fell farther back and Quinn went with it. His impressive torso came over her enough for her to slip lower against the arm of the sofa.

Clairy uncurled her legs and stretched them over Quinn's thighs as her arms wrapped around him and her fingers gripped his back more firmly.

Kneading, almost burrowing into him, she gave him a clue to what her own body was starting to yearn for.

He didn't seem to need much of a hint, though. He let the couch's arm brace her head and trailed that hand down one shoulder to her arm, crossing from there to the outer swell of her breast, lingering as if awaiting permission.

Clairy gave it with the faintest of pivots. Quinn

took the invitation without hesitation, bringing his big hand to cup her breast completely then.

He wasn't just a fantastic kisser—he had a magic touch that kindled a fire in her.

A quiet sound she'd never heard herself make sent him a message and his hand dropped from her breast to the blouse's buttons at her side.

Fastened, those buttons made the V neckline demure. But as he opened the top button, the V widened. And widened more when he undid the next two, leaving only the bottom button to keep her shirt from falling completely open.

Then that hand went to her collarbone instead of to her breast, inspiring a minor complaint to rumble from Clairy's throat as she taunted his tongue, tip to tip, with some audacity.

She felt him smile just before he retook control of that kiss and let his hand sluice downward, his fingers easing inside the cup of her bra to finally give her that unfettered embrace of his strong, adept hand on her naked breast.

He caressed, stroked, squeezed, gently tugged and pinched her flesh—her breast seemed to expand, and her nipple turned to stone in his palm.

With his mouth still in control of that kiss and her, Clairy's body slid even more down the sofa side, more fully across Quinn's lap, where she discovered that she was not the only one of them nearly going out of her mind with wanting even more.

But where? Here on her office couch? In her father's memorial-library building?

Maybe if they were longtime lovers looking for a new titillation.

But for the first time?

The thought of that put just enough of a damper on things for something else to creep into her mind— was this wise at all? Was this something she should do and let go all the way to the conclusion her body was screaming for?

Her body *was* screaming for it.

And she could feel beneath her hip that his was, too.

But this was still Quinn Camden—was she absolutely positive she should take this step with him?

Plus, she was so fresh out of her marriage, and should phase one of her postdivorce life go this far? Should she let it if she had any doubt at all?

Whether Quinn read her mind or felt some amount of withdrawal—or had the same hesitations himself— he stopped kissing her just then.

"Okay...we shouldn't be doing this..." he said, leaving Clairy still unsure what had caused him to stop.

Still, she said, "Probably not..." as the shadow of doubt grew.

It was only then that Quinn stole one last stroke of her breast and drew his hand out from under her bra, pulling the ruffled edges of her blouse back in place.

Clairy refastened the buttons as she sat up straight

and edged off Quinn's lap, turning just enough to put her feet on the floor.

Quinn dropped his head onto the sofa back, closed his eyes and took a deep breath, then sighed it out. "You're getting to me, Clairy..." he said in a gravelly voice.

"Or maybe you're getting to me," she countered, making him laugh.

"God, what's happening here?" he muttered, sounding as confused as she felt.

"I don't know," Clairy confessed.

"We're supposed to hate each other."

"It'd be a lot safer," she said, thinking out loud.

"We're only together for a few days..."

"And you're one of those macho military men," she added, unable to keep the attraction she had to him out of that criticism.

"One of those macho military men who swore I was taking a hiatus to figure out what the hell I'm doing with relationships before I screw up another one..."

"It's all just complicated," Clairy said, unsure what he meant about a hiatus and figuring out what he was doing with relationships.

"Complicated..." he repeated, as if he needed that reinforced. "Complicated enough that we need to think it through," Quinn said, sounding much more rational than Clairy felt, until he added, "Don't we?"

"I think so," she said with the same combination of certainty and uncertainty.

Quinn sighed again, this time with resignation and disappointment. Then he opened his eyes, raised his head and nodded. "Okay..."

Another moment passed before he took a third deep breath, sighed once more and stood. "Let's get out of here before I can't make myself," he said, turning to offer his hand.

Clairy took it because she couldn't deny herself, even though she knew it was dangerous to make contact again and had to fight the inclination to pull him back down to her.

Then they left her office and silently descended the library's stairs.

At the front entrance, Clairy turned off the lights. But before she could open the doors, Quinn used the hand he was holding to pull her into another kiss so heated that this time what flashed through her mind was what it would be like to just go ahead and make love on the library floor.

But then he ended that kiss, too, opened one of the double doors and held it for her to go out ahead of him.

Clairy locked up after them and they returned to Quinn's truck, still saying nothing, merely letting the night air help dissipate what was still alive between them.

Quinn held the passenger door for her, too, before he got behind the wheel to drive them back to her house.

Her house, her front walkway, her porch...where she toyed with the idea of asking him in.

But she didn't have the chance before he kissed her again—as chastely as an altar boy—then told her to let him know when she wanted him to help her move the display cases the next day, and left her to let herself into her house.

Where wanting was definitely still on her mind. And what her body was still overheated with.

But it had nothing at all to do with display cases.

And everything to do with the man who seemed like the worst choice she could possibly make...

Chapter Seven

"I love that dress!" Marabeth said as she and Clairy went into Marabeth's small apartment kitchen Friday evening.

"Thanks. Me, too," Clairy said of the gray-and-white windowpane dress that was tight-fitting through the bodice and flared from her waist to her knees.

"Kind of sexy, almost off-the-shoulder—you're putting me to shame in my shorts and T-shirt," her friend complained.

"Quinn and I worked all day at the library dealing with the display cases. I had to go home and shower, and I just wanted something light and airy tonight."

Feminine—that was what she'd told herself instead of labeling it as sexy.

"And with your hair down and your makeup all done... After hobnobbing with Jared and his rich friends in Denver, you may have to tone it down for plain old Merritt salmon-on-the-barbecue summer dinners."

Clairy didn't want to tell her friend that it hadn't been this dinner that had been on her mind when she'd dressed for tonight. She didn't want to tell Marabeth that—like always lately—Quinn had been what she was thinking about.

Quinn, and the way Thursday night had ended. And all the things that ending had left unfinished. And that the only thing she'd been able to think about since then was whether or not she should let those things be finished...

"At least Quinn just wore jeans and a T-shirt," Marabeth said, casting a glance across the room and out the patio door to where he and Marabeth's fiancé were standing on the small cement slab that was the apartment's patio, in front of the outdoor grill, beers in hand.

Marabeth was right—Quinn was dressed casually. But even so, the sight of him in jeans and a navy blue polo shirt still increased her already whetted appetite.

"Is this—tonight—okay?" Marabeth asked then, sounding tentative. "Having the two of you here together?"

The newly engaged couple had invited Clairy and Quinn to Marabeth's apartment for dinner.

"We wanted to thank you for the party," Marabeth went on, "and Brad wanted to have Quinn over before he leaves town again, so we thought if we could have you both at the same time…"

"It's fine, no big deal," Clairy answered her friend.

"How's it going between the two of you?" Marabeth asked. "I never saw you together at the party, but I know he was still there when I left. And tonight he drove you?"

"Seemed silly to take two cars."

"Because you're on friendlier terms…?" Marabeth queried.

"We've been working together so much we've sort of had to be."

There wasn't much to that statement, and yet it seemed to be exactly what Marabeth wanted to hear. "I knew it!" she said victoriously. "I told Brad when we left your house Wednesday night and Quinn didn't that *something* was going on!"

"Something has been going on—we've been *working* together. And Wednesday night Quinn stayed to help finish the cleanup and take out the party trash," Clairy said.

But her friend wasn't accepting that it was as low-key as Clairy was trying to make it sound. "And then?" Marabeth urged.

Clairy knew denial wasn't going to fool her bloodhound best friend, so she gave up the ghost and just smiled.

"I knew it! I knew it! I knew it!" Marabeth's exclamation was loud enough to stop the conversation outside and draw the men's attention.

"Everything okay in there?" her fiancé asked.

"Just fine," Marabeth called back, delight in her tone and in her face. Then to Clairy, she said quietly, "How friendly has it gotten?"

"Enough for me to learn that you *might* be right that he's not the same as he was before—"

"Like Brad. I told you!" Marabeth interrupted her with more triumph.

"Plus, I've gotten to know Quinn a little better and learned a few things that explain some of what he did as a kid. And he's bent over backward apologizing."

"And now you like him!" Marabeth concluded, sounding like a teenager.

"Now I don't think I hate him anymore." That was all Clairy would concede.

Marabeth shook her head vigorously. "You dressed up for him tonight!" she accused. "Have you already slept with him? Did the two of you come here straight from bed? Did you get all dressed up so it didn't look like that?"

"No!" Clairy scoffed before her friend could dig in any deeper.

"But you *want* to sleep with him!"

Clairy finally caved and confessed under her

breath, "So bad," giving up all pretenses and making her friend laugh.

"Then why haven't you?"

"Come on, really? There are a million reasons."

"But if you want to, that's the only reason that counts."

Clairy sighed, laughed and shook her head at that oversimplification.

"I'm serious," Marabeth said. "Just do it for fun—after Jared and seven years of uninspired, scheduled sex that had to be over in time for the financial report? You've earned it!"

Clairy and Marabeth had shared every intimate detail of their lives since they were children, including that. And especially after Clairy complaining to Jared hadn't accomplished anything, and she'd grown more and more disappointed and frustrated. Which had led to venting to her friend.

"Is that really me, though?" Clairy said. "I'm barely divorced. A week ago I still counted Quinn as my sworn enemy. Plus, there's nowhere for anything between us to go, and knowing that, wouldn't it end up seeming kind of shallow and maybe even…yucky? I mean—"

"I know. We've both always needed there to be a full-blown relationship, the potential for a future, love—or at least being on the verge of love…"

They really had been discussing this subject since puberty.

"So let's look at it like that," Marabeth suggested. "Maybe things between the two of you *could* go somewhere…"

Clairy shook her head again, a slow, definitively negative shake that allowed for no possibility.

Despite that, Marabeth went on. "What if the line between love and hate *is* thin and the two of you have crossed it? What if your dad's death is destiny bringing you together? Think how great that would be! We could do this—" Marabeth glanced out the patio door again "—we could all live here in Merritt, two best friends married to two best friends. The four of us could have dinner *every* Friday night. We could raise kids together who could all end up best friends, too—or maybe they'd fall in love and get married to each other and make us all one big—"

"Oh, we've entered fantasyland!" Clairy said.

"Stranger things have happened."

"I don't think they have," Clairy said. "Even if Quinn might have changed, he hasn't changed *that* much. He's still my father's marine mirror image—a dyed-in-the-wool *forever* marine—"

"And exactly the kind of person you swore you would never get involved with when you grew up," Marabeth said, repeating what Clairy had told her numerous times.

"The kind of person I pretty much already married, which means I had to learn all over again that it's what I don't want, because if that fantasy of yours played out with Quinn, I'd either be on a military base somewhere hoping it might give me ten more minutes with him, or here alone—raising kids alone—and not even getting that ten minutes. No, thanks."

Marabeth deflated. "I know you're right." It took only a moment, though, before she brightened again. "But then I'm back to saying just have some fun now, while he *is* around."

Brad poked his head in the open patio door. "Platter—we're getting close," he announced.

Marabeth took a serving dish over to him and kissed him, then returned to the kitchen cubicle and Clairy.

Only when she was sure her fiancé was fully outside and talking to Quinn did she go on. "If you were ever going to have a one-night stand, this is the perfect setup, isn't it?" Marabeth said in a confidential tone. "The guy is sizzling hot with a body that doesn't end. You want to. You already know there's no future in anything with him, so you don't have any illusions about anything coming of it. He'll disappear any day and you may never see him again—or at least probably won't see him again for years—so you don't have to worry about being embarrassed or awkward or anything, if or when you meet up again. And it's a great way to put Jared behind you, take that first step at moving on."

"Postdivorce phase one," Clairy said with a laugh,

explaining that she'd already considered most of what Marabeth was saying.

"So you're gonna do it," Marabeth said optimistically.

"I'm not sure. And I don't think he is, either."

"So seduce him," Marabeth whispered.

Clairy laughed once more, but she didn't commit to anything.

As tempting as it was to consider that one-night stand with Quinn, she still wasn't sure she should.

Or could.

Because what if she did take that leap and *didn't* come away from it as unaffected and detached as her friend thought she would?

"Am I missing something?" Quinn said on the way back to Clairy's house when Friday evening with their friends had ended. "How come Marabeth wouldn't let you *not* take that bottle of wine and kept telling you to go home and open it tonight?"

Quick lie, quick lie, come up with a quick lie, Clairy...

"She thought you and I should celebrate burying the hatchet to work together on the memorial and finishing the project."

"Ah…" he said, seeming to accept that. "So you told her you'd buried the hatchet?" he asked, sounding very interested to hear that.

"I told her that she might be right, that you—and

maybe Brad, too—aren't still the creep you used to be."

Quinn laughed. "Faint praise but I'll take it and be grateful."

There was a moment's lull that Clairy hoped put to rest his curiosity about the wine Marabeth had really given her to encourage having some *fun* tonight.

Then he said, "If you think we might not still be creeps, does that mean you're feeling better about Brad?"

"I'm hoping for the best," Clairy allowed. "Marabeth is going to marry him no matter what I think, and I don't want to see any marriage fail."

"There's always that risk, though. Relationships are tough."

"Spoken from experience?" she asked.

"To be honest, relationships have been really easy for me—even the two that went on for a while. Until the end of them, anyway. But, apparently, they have been tougher than I ever realized for whoever I've been involved with."

"Let me guess—they're easy for you because you enjoy the fruits of the relationships, then go on about your business. You get deployed or leave for trainings or missions or whatever. But the women you've been involved with are left behind, left hanging, waiting, worrying, and as alone as if they weren't involved with anyone at all."

"Well, yeah. But that's all a given, being involved with anyone in the military," Quinn said. "My two bad breakups put a whole lot more blame on me than on the military, and after this last deal with Mac, it got me to thinking—"

"Were they women marines that my father tried to push out?"

"No, both the women were civilians. Rachel was a legal secretary and Laine was a paramedic. Neither of them ever even met Mac. But after having my eyes opened to the way Mac saw women—and looking at the complaints against me through that lens—I decided that maybe I'd better figure out if being involved with me has had its own special downside."

Was that why he was taking a hiatus before he screwed up another relationship, what he'd said last night?

But Merritt was a small town and it had only been a short drive from Marabeth's apartment, so he'd piqued Clairy's curiosity again just as he pulled his truck up to the curb in front of her house. And there was no way Clairy could just end the evening and leave it at that.

She held up the bottle her friend had forced on her as they'd left and said, "So, wine…" as an invitation to come inside and tell her more.

Quinn's only answer was a smile before he opened his door and got out.

Clairy got out, too, and met him to walk up to the house.

She'd meant to turn on the air-conditioning before leaving tonight, and remembered only after unlocking the front door, when they went into the heat and stuffiness of her house.

"It's miserable in here," she complained as she turned on the air now. "Mim and Harry brought her old patio glider over this morning—they didn't like the look of it with Harry's outdoor furniture. It's in the backyard again and I left the lights from the party up, so why don't we take the wine out there?"

"Good idea."

Clairy gave Quinn the job of uncorking the bottle as she kicked off her sandals and got two glasses. Once he'd poured the wine, she led the way out the rear door.

She'd used string lights with small white round globes to add to the festivity of the party, and they still made a nice canopy over the yard.

The cushioned, love-seat-sized glider that was against the house was comfortable, if not contemporary. The unoiled metal base squeaked when they both sat down, and the seat unavoidably moved backward until they were settled, facing each other.

"Okay, explain how what you found out about my father triggered something about your private life," she prompted.

"It goes without saying that Mac was the biggest

influence on me—from the time I was a little kid. When I found out what he was doing to women marines, it kind of opened a curtain on what he thought of the opposite sex in general." Quinn tried his wine, seemingly buying himself a moment.

Similar to when he'd told her about her father's misdeeds Thursday night, Clairy could see again that it was difficult for him to speak ill of her father, that it was a struggle he waged with himself.

Then he said, "You came to mind, and for the first time, I actually thought about the way he'd always treated you. I don't know why—knowing Mim, knowing how he was raised, it shouldn't have been true of him—but Mac deeply *believed* that there was something that made men better, more important, more valuable all the way around, than any woman."

Clairy breathed a wry sigh at that. "I had that same thought last night when you told me what he'd been doing. It kind of helped me to think that it wasn't only me... I've always thought it was..."

"It definitely wasn't only you. But the thing is, it got me to thinking about the way I'd treated you when we were kids and about the way I might have followed Mac's lead—"

"It seemed okay to you to be a jerk to me, to shove me aside to get to my father, because I was just a *girl* and not as good as you," Clairy surmised.

Quinn flinched. "It was never a conscious thought.

It's never been a conscious thought about any woman. But your dad was—"

"Your idol, your role model, everything you wanted to be, and if that was how he saw women, maybe it rubbed off on you."

"That's what I wondered about. Beginning with you and the way I treated you when we were kids."

"It *was* what my father modeled for you from the day you showed up at our door," Clairy confirmed, looking at the situation like that herself now. "I actually remember that morning like it was yesterday. He was reading his newspaper, ignoring me. But when you got there and said you wanted to be a marine just like him, he folded it and put it down, and suddenly he was interested in what you had to say."

"Again, Clairy, I'm sorry," Quinn said contritely. "But, yeah, Mac did act like you were just…a pet or a piece of furniture—something we didn't need to take into consideration even when you were trying to get in on his training me, or when you wanted to watch his war movies with us…"

Clairy nodded, but this time instead of getting into that part of this, she was more interested in how this had translated into Quinn's view and treatment of the women in his life.

He seemed to sense that and went on. "Even though I never consciously thought I was better than or more important than any woman, I can see where

Mac's influence may have colored the way I've always gone about things with women—"

"With very little regard for them?" Another guess.

"Possibly. I know personal relationships have never had priority with me—"

"Long- or short-term ones?"

"Any of them," he admitted somewhat under his breath. "Short-term were just numbers I called or texted when I felt like it. If there was no answer, I called or texted the next number on the list—"

"Oh, nice!" she chided.

"They were doing the same thing with me," he claimed.

"And the long-terms?"

"I guess I didn't recognize that things were much different with those," he acknowledged, sobering as if thinking back on the more serious relationships really was giving him pause now.

"With Rachel," he said, "it lasted about a year, and I thought we were doing okay—I was stationed in Georgia then. After dating steadily for two months, I needed to leave on assignment for a few weeks. She invited me to stay at her place when I got back, to stay with her every time I was going to be back rather than staying on base. I thought she was being...you know, practical. I'd made it clear that I'd be in and out. She seemed to accept that, and she said she wanted to keep things going even under those circumstances, to be together whenever I was in town. I figured she just figured that it was nicer to have her place to come back to than the base, that it was for convenience."

"But she saw it differently—as the two of you living together," Clairy suggested.

"She didn't say that outright in the invitation, but she did when things blew up—she said me moving in took the relationship to another level. But I hadn't seen that…" He shook his head as if he still didn't completely see it. "I guess she expected me to propose or something… Hell, I don't know exactly. I just know I thought we were on the same page, and I didn't think it was headed anywhere close to marriage. But when things exploded, she said she'd given me hints and signs and signals, that she'd said things that—if I'd given her even a second thought—I would have caught."

His sigh sounded frustrated. "The bottom line was that she wanted more, and she'd believed when I moved in that she had the right to expect it… But I was…oblivious. And it all came to a head when I found her in bed with some other guy—"

"Oh… She wasn't expecting you?"

"She knew I was coming. She just wanted to rub my nose in the fact that she had someone else. She said it was what I deserved, that it was what it took to get me to notice her, to notice what was going on with her because I took her for granted."

That did sound like Clairy's complaint with her father, but it seemed as if Quinn was finding his way with this and she thought it might be better to just let that happen on its own rather than point out the similarity.

"I thought setting me up to walk in on her in bed with somebody else was taking it too far," Quinn continued. "But thinking about it since Camp Lejeune and Mac... I don't know... Rachel was right that she wasn't uppermost in my mind at any point, that I wasn't paying enough attention to anything she said or did or signaled for it to register. I did enjoy her company, but when I didn't have it, it didn't...bother me."

"You could take her or leave her?" Clairy asked to put it in simpler terms.

He shrugged, and it seemed to have a tinge of guilt to it. "I could. And did," he confessed. "After she'd had her say, I packed up and left without feeling anything but...mostly confusion at how I'd missed so much. But she was crying and throwing things—she said she wanted to hurt me the way I'd hurt her—"

"And that just shocked you," Clairy said.

"That I'd hurt her? It did. I didn't think I was doing anything wrong. I definitely didn't *want* to hurt her."

And it was apparent that he was genuinely perplexed by the fact that he had.

"Then there was Laine," he went on. "So-o-o much worse..."

Enough for him to need a drink of his wine before going on.

"I met her right after Rachel," he began. "I was

with her until just before going to Camp Lejeune to see Mac—*twenty months of her life...*" He seemed to be repeating what had been said to him.

"Almost two years," Clairy observed.

"Again, I was in and out, so it didn't seem like that and probably didn't add up to that much actual time together. But Laine hadn't seen anyone else, so—"

"Had you?"

"No. I liked her. I was fine seeing only her."

Obviously without putting much thought into it...

"Were you *fine* seeing only her just because she always answered when hers was the first number you called when you got to town? So you didn't have to bother with the next number on the list?"

"Don't make me out to be a dog," Quinn said defensively.

Okay, maybe there had been a bit of a bite to that. And it wasn't really fair, she decided, because since his personal life took a back seat to his career, she had no doubt he didn't devote enough time or energy to dating to juggle women.

But before Clairy could retract what she'd said, he went on.

"I didn't mistreat anyone...intentionally, at least. I was just... Like I said, relationships weren't my priority. But I liked Laine, and after a couple of months seeing only her and then having to be gone, if she hadn't answered when I got back, I'd have called again and again until I got her. I wouldn't have moved on to the next number."

Clairy thought he likely saw that as the highest of regard when it came to women and relationships, but she didn't say it. She could tell that he really was suffering remorse now for doing what he hadn't seen as wrong at the time he was doing it.

"So the two of you were exclusive, too. For twenty months," Clairy said to encourage him to go on.

"Without living together—I'd learned that lesson, at least. But Laine got pregnant."

That was a bombshell Clairy hadn't seen coming.

"Do you have a kid? Or is there someone out there pregnant with your baby?" she asked, in full-blown alarm.

"No! The pregnancy was an accident. She didn't even know she *was* pregnant until pain sent her to the emergency room and they told her it was... I hope I have this word right—ectopic?"

"The embryo was in her fallopian tube," Clairy said.

"She had to go into surgery right then and they had to take the whole deal—the tube and all. I was working, busy. I'd turned off my phone, left it in my desk drawer so she couldn't reach me. I didn't see her messages, her texts, until it was all over with. A friend of hers had taken her to the hospital..." he confessed ruefully.

Clairy couldn't help feeling sympathy for these two women who had gotten in over their heads with him. After all the pain her father's neglect and disregard of her had caused, she identified with them and understood what it was to be so let down by a man who was more intent on something other than them.

But she could also tell that Quinn was agonizing over what he was just realizing about himself and his actions, and she didn't want to rub salt into his wounds, so she didn't say anything at all.

He went on even without any input from her.

"Laine was through with me when I finally did get to her. She said she'd wasted twenty months of her life on me, that her chances of having kids had been reduced and all for what... She'd been hanging on, hoping it would get better—hoping *I* would get better—but that the whole mess had opened her eyes and she knew she'd never mean as much to me as the marines did, that she'd never been that important to me, that she was so *un*important to me that she hadn't even known where I was or how to reach me other than by the cell phone I'd turned off—"

"You'd hurt her, too," Clairy interrupted, but mildly and with understanding that this had caught him as unaware as had learning how the other woman felt.

"Again, not on purpose," he said. "And at the time it happened I was sorry it had all gone down the way it had, but I still wrote off most of Laine's reaction to things other than me."

Just as her father would have done.

"But now?" Clairy asked.

"Now I'm afraid I might not be much different than the worst of Mac, even though I've lived my life trying to be the best of him…"

So not only had Quinn become disillusioned by his idol, but he was also ashamed of what the negative side of that idol's influence might have created in him.

"I think just coming to all this makes you a better man than my father was," Clairy said honestly. "And maybe it'll lead to a better, more rounded life than he had. Maybe since you know now where you've failed, you won't do it again and you can actually *have* a personal life—because whether or not my father ever realized it or cared, he didn't."

"Which brings me to the rest of what I'm trying to figure out," Quinn said more to himself than to her.

"Whether or not you *want* a personal life that might interfere with being the kind of marine my father was," Clairy ventured.

Quinn's eyebrows arched. "Oh, you're too smart…" he said with a wry laugh, letting her know her guess had been correct.

And since it had, she took a leap and said, "Speaking from my father's personal life, if you have to be the marine he was, look for a woman—like my mother, like Mim—willing to accept it, excuse it. But don't bring kids into it. Like your two long-term relationships, kids can't help hoping and trying and working for more, and then being hurt when they can't get it."

"And that's pretty rotten for the kid," he said compassionately, clearly referring to her.

That compassion brought a warmth to his eyes and they held hers for long enough to cause her to think he was finished talking. That they might be moving in that other direction she still wasn't sure the night should take.

But then he seemed to pull himself out of the moment. He took a drink of his wine and returned to talking, just not about himself.

"Okay, I've told you the dark secret of my mistakes. Let me hear yours."

"Who said I have any dark secrets or mistakes?"

"You've dropped some crumbs, some teasers," he accused. "Tell me who got you to the altar and how. And why it didn't work."

She'd heard that talking about the ex was a sure-fire way to put a damper on anything involving another man.

So maybe this was a good night for it...

"His name is Jared Byers—he's a financial and real-estate whiz in Denver. We met at an event I did to raise money for the Jenkins Foundation. I married him after a whirlwind three-month courtship and it lasted for seven years."

"Hmm... I think you left out all the important parts with that version and I'm not letting you off the hook," Quinn said of her summary. "So you were married seven years. Was it the seven-year itch that wrecked it?"

"If the seven-year itch means cheating, then no, neither of us did that. If it means seven years into a marriage is when some reassessing might happen, when someone might reevaluate, might need things to change course, then yes."

"Which of you did all that?"

"Me."

Quinn smiled broadly. "Straightforward taking responsibility—I like that. Now explain."

His reaction made her inclined to be more candid, but first she set her half-empty wineglass on the small table on her side of the glider.

"Jared has it all—he came from money that he turned into much, much more money in real estate and in two private mortgage loan groups he heads, so he's rich, charming—when he wants to be—handsome—"

As she settled again to face Quinn, she thought that her ex came up short in a comparison of his looks and Quinn's. But she didn't say that. Instead, she said, "And he swept me off my feet."

"That was bad?" Quinn asked, interpreting her tone.

"It ended up making me feel kind of stupid, like I'd fallen for a con man—"

"He was a con man?" Quinn asked with the same level of alarm she'd had when she'd worried he might have a child or have left a pregnant girlfriend.

"No, he's on the up-and-up. He's just a very high-flier. He went—goes—after things full speed ahead, and while I didn't know it until much later, he'd decided it was time for a wife. I guess I fit his qualifications, so when we met I was what he went after—"

"Full speed ahead," Quinn said, echoing her words. "But you don't think he did that because he had feelings for you? You think he just did it to acquire a wife—like a piece of property?"

"Without it taking him away from work for long," she confirmed. "And *acquired* is pretty accurate. It turned out that I was more of an acquisition than anything, and once I was on his list of assets—"

"He had to have feelings for you, though," Quinn insisted.

"Do you think my father *had feelings* for me?" Clairy countered.

"You were his daughter," Quinn answered, as if there was no question.

"And my mom was his wife. But when she died I never saw him shed a single tear—"

"I don't think that was something he would have *let* you see."

"When I got upset he got mad at me—he didn't have any trouble showing *that*. He said a McKinnon didn't cry. My mom dying in a car wreck was sad, but we had to see it through."

"But looking back on it as an adult, do you honestly believe he didn't *have* any feelings, or can you see that the man Mac was wouldn't have shown them?"

"That was Mim's excuse for him. But it just seemed to me like he didn't have much in the way of feelings for anything but the marines…and you, as the son he wanted. And I'm not sure Jared has feelings for anything except *his* work. I know that's what gives him a rush that nothing else does. But until we were actually married, he made it seem as if I gave him that same kind of rush."

"I can't imagine that you didn't," Quinn said, as if he wouldn't accept anything else. "So how did he sweep you off your feet?"

"He made it seem as if he couldn't get enough of me. There were a whole lot of picnic lunches, and dinners that were all candles and starlight and private dining rooms. There were chartered planes to weekends in Paris and Rome and London and Switzerland. There were flowers and candy and gifts. He called and texted dozens of times a day to tell me how much he missed me, how all he wanted was to be with me, how he couldn't wait until he was… It was as if *I'd* swept *him* off his feet. I didn't know it at the time, but when Jared wants something, he devotes himself to getting it. He's like a heat-seeking missile—nothing is going to stop him."

"My mother would have been impressed?"

Clairy chuckled. "It sounds like she could have raised him."

"And how did you feel about him?"

"I wasn't *instantly* in love with him, but feelings did develop fairly soon. I did fall in love with him and I started to believe there might be something to all those it-happened-so-fast-and-lasted-forever love stories. So when he proposed three months after we'd met—"

"You said yes."

"I did," she said with some self-disgust. "Jared didn't want a long engagement, and with the money he could spend to get things done in a hurry—which he was willing and eager to do—we were married two weeks later."

"A small wedding or—"

"A blowout. Three hundred people—just not my father, who wouldn't come even to give me away because he was doing something more important..." But they weren't discussing her father, so Clairy let it go and went on. "It *was* a beautiful wedding. With so many of Jared's wealthy friends there that the fundraiser in me was screaming to pass the hat. It took everything I had to just sit back and be the bride," she joked wryly to lighten the tone.

"I'm almost afraid to ask what kind of honeymoon Mr. Romance took you on."

"A week living like royalty in Banff."

"Then home to Denver?"

"To Jared's penthouse."

"Then what—he just stopped with the sweeping you off your feet and went back to business?"

"Pretty much. It was kind of a shock. A big project had come up for him two days before the wedding. He'd mostly put it on hold through the honeymoon—although he did spend more time on his phone than I'd expected. He warned me that he was going to have to dive in when we got back. I just had no idea what *diving in* really meant."

"What did it mean?"

"He worked until ten or eleven at night, seven days a week. Sometimes he didn't come home at all for days and just sent his assistant for changes of clothes. I knew the over-the-top courting wouldn't go on, but I didn't think that…well, that I'd been just another acquisition and no more thought needed to be put into me from then on. That for the next seven years I'd be to Jared what I'd always been to my father—incidental. That I'd just be The Wife."

"Just *The Wife*?" Quinn queried, trolling for an explanation.

"The person who ran the home front, took care of Jared and his home and his home life the way his assistant at work took care of him and everything he needed there. I was less *his wife* and more *The Wife*—it was like a job I'd been hired to do, not a relationship. I was who showed up on his arm at any event he needed or wanted to attend—which was particularly important because I learned about six months into the marriage that that was what made him decide he should have a wife—"

"Having a built-in date for parties and dinners?"

"He was sick and tired of being The Most Eligible Bachelor—he'd actually been named that on the cover of a Denver magazine. Single women preyed on him, all his friends badgered him with setups to help him find someone, and they insisted he take time away from work to meet whoever they had in mind. There were even a few clients—important ones—who wanted him to go out with their single daughter or niece and tried to make it part of their deal. I guess that's what brought him to me—a client really pushed him to date the client's daughter and Jared begged off and lost the project to someone else."

"So he decided to get himself a token wife? It was a business decision?"

"That's what I overheard in a ladies' room when a group of wives from his inner circle didn't know I was in one of the stalls."

"Aww, Clairy..." Quinn said sympathetically. "Did you ask him if that was true? Did he at least deny it and get rid of that inner circle?"

"Neither of those things. He did insist that it was just lucky for him that I came along when I did, but it didn't help much."

"You'd married 'Mac without a uniform' and nothing changed."

Clairy shrugged her concession to the truth in that statement. "Jared wasn't as gruff as my father. He was generous—just not with his time. He was considerate enough to have his assistant keep me up-to-date on when he'd be home, when he wouldn't be, when he'd be going out of town on business, when he had social obligations I needed to put on my calendar, too. When I got dressed for those social obligations, he complimented me... The marriage was just...cut-and-dried, mechanical..."

"That had to be a *huge* letdown after the whirlwind."

"The whirlwind definitely hadn't prepared me, no."

"But you stuck around for seven years?"

"When it started to sink in that his work was the be-all and end-all to him, like my father, I guess I did what I'd done growing up—for a long time, I tried to get back Jared's attention in any way I could. When that didn't work, I thought maybe I should try playing on his field—I thought that if I was really fluent in what he did, he might talk to me about it. So I watched and read all his financial reports, all his real-estate stuff, tried getting him to tell me about his projects. But that just irritated him the same way it had when I tried to get my father to include me in your training—he saw it as something that interfered with his focus."

"Did sex play a role?"

Clairy's initial thought was that Quinn was asking about her sex *life*. Then she realized he was referring to her father rejecting her because she wasn't male.

Her own misunderstanding made her laugh. "For a minute, I thought you were asking something else…"

Quinn smiled. "You thought I was asking how things were in bed…"

"To answer the real question—yes and no. Jared wasn't sexist in terms of believing that women couldn't be more than homemakers. There were women he worked with whom he trusted, respected. But he definitely put me in one role and left me there. He even saw my job with the Jenkins Foundation more as a little hobby that could occupy me when he wasn't around. I was The Wife and he didn't want me playing any role but that."

"And you still didn't bolt when you figured that out?"

She shrugged. "The whirlwind *had* made me fall in love with him," she reminded Quinn. "So when everything I tried failed, I spent a lot of time just working at accepting that things were the way they were. Plus, I did have my job—I was free to put in a lot of extra hours and Jared *was* great for fundraising. I had the best list of the moneyed elite in the state and access to all of them. His connections also gave me inside pipelines to things for my vets that no one else had—"

"The good with the bad?"

"That was how I tried to look at it. I also told myself that after the way I grew up, I was kind of uniquely qualified for what the marriage turned out to be. Plus," she added somewhat sheepishly, "I didn't want to be the story where I was swept off my feet into an instant marriage that ended as fast as it started. And there was my father... I didn't want to look impetuous and flighty and add a divorce to the rest of what a disappointment I was to him. So I just tried to take the marriage for what it was and be content with it while I held on to the hope that it would somehow get better—"

"Like Laine," Quinn said somberly. "Only Mr. Whirlwind didn't get any better, either. So what made you reach your limit like Laine did and decide enough was enough?"

"It was last Christmas. It was the same as every Christmas had been since we were married. Nice, very formal and stuffy because Jared didn't like *homey*— that's what he called what I wanted and he said it as if I was embarrassingly out of style. As always, we had invitations to A-list parties and dinners, concerts, plays, the ballet, and Jared would fit in a few that had business connections..." She shrugged once more. "It was nice enough," she repeated. "But I was so homesick I was miserable. It all seemed superficial and empty, cold and impersonal. I wanted to be with Mim. I wanted a Merritt Christmas with the ice sculptures and the Christmas Festival. With the cookie competition and exchanges. With the caroling and the church choir. With Marabeth. With all the *hominess*. And with a husband who was actually enjoying it with me, not sitting in the seat next to me at the symphony engrossed in what he was doing on his phone." Clairy sighed. "And I realized that I also wanted kids…"

"For the first time?"

"I always saw myself with a family, and I assumed we'd get there, even though we never really talked about it—Jared's friends had kids and that seemed to be what he took his cues from for a home life. And last Christmas it just hit me hard that I wanted that next step—"

"Even with the way things were?" Quinn asked, as if he doubted the wisdom in that.

"I guess I tapped into my old habit of trying to somehow make it better. I started to picture becoming a family and that family engaging Jared. I saw us getting out of high-rise living, moving into a house, having the life I'd thought I was going to have. So on Christmas night I cornered him in the bathroom on his way to taking a shower so he didn't have anything that could take his attention away. And I told him what I wanted for the New Year."

"It didn't go over well," Quinn said.

"Jared was calm. He took it in stride. He said he wasn't thrilled with the family idea, but if I wanted to have a baby, it was up to me."

Quinn laughed mirthlessly. "Was he planning to be the father?"

"More like the sperm donor and sponsor. He said if I *had* to do it there was a bigger penthouse he had his eye on that could probably accommodate a nursery, but that I should know he wasn't changing anything beyond that. He definitely wasn't moving outside of the city or working any differently or any less. He said I could hire a nanny, but there was no way he was doing bottle duty, diaper duty, or getting up in the middle of the night for anything. He said he wasn't pushing a stroller through a park or going to Little League games—in case I had any illusions about that. He wasn't going to play Santa or the Easter Bunny, birthday parties would be my thing, not his…" Clairy realized her tone had begun to mimic Jared's the way Quinn's had echoed his former girlfriend's, so she cut herself off.

She merely did what she'd done with Jared—she got as calm as her ex had been.

"And that was it for me," she said resolutely. "I looked at him while he dictated his terms and it occurred to me that somewhere along the way my feelings for him had fizzled. I wasn't even angry. I realized how much Jared was like my father, and that after my father, after seven years with Jared, I was done accepting, adapting, trying to change anything with that kind of man. I was done *being* with that kind of man—the kind of man I hadn't wanted in the first place." Clairy sighed again. "I said no to his terms, that it was over between us. The day after Christmas, he rented the bigger penthouse to try it out and accommodate a separation. He moved there by New Year's. I filed for divorce the week after that."

"He didn't look for a middle ground to keep you? He didn't get upset?"

She shook her head. "Like my father, the only way was his way. Lawyers worked everything out—there was a prenuptial agreement because I'd come into the marriage with so much less than he had. We didn't have kids to battle over, so it was all pretty simple—"

"When was it final?"

"Not until last week—Jared apparently liked the structure of having The Wife, because by March he had someone new—"

"Did he do the whirlwind deal again?"

"No, he actually wooed that client he'd lost when he'd refused to date the client's daughter—"

"Oh, jeez, he hooked up with the daughter to get the client back?"

"And cemented that business relationship in the process—two birds with one stone. They were engaged in May and he needed the divorce to be final, or he'd still probably be too busy to sign the papers."

"What about you?"

Clairy shook her head. "I was kind of surprised that there weren't even enough feelings left to make any of it hurt. Jared had been gone so much, he'd been so distant when he *was* around, that it was hard to tell when he wasn't living there anymore. Nothing much changed except that I didn't have to cater to him."

"So it was more like putting in notice to leave a job you'd had for seven years?"

"I never looked at it like that but it sort of was," Clairy said with another laugh. "I wish I would have thought of that earlier. Maybe I wouldn't have felt so guilty for *not* being more upset. And as for The Wife Number Two, I just hope she has more idea what she's getting into than I did."

Quinn's expression became reflective. "I guess you could say that Mac was a bad influence on both of us when it comes to our personal lives."

"I guess you could," Clairy agreed.

"But now I've woken up and will be more careful, and you won't make the same mistake again," Quinn said.

"Uniform or no uniform," Clairy said firmly.

"I'm sorry that happened to you," Quinn said compassionately. He leaned forward and reached across her to put his half-full wineglass on the table with hers, and when he straightened up again, he was nearer than he'd been before.

Looking more raptly into her eyes, he added, "I think the guy did have feelings for you, though—

even if he didn't show it or beg you not to end it or try to find a compromise to keep you."

"What makes you think that?"

"He may have made the decision to find himself The Wife Number Two so he could get his client back and avoid the nuisance of fix-ups again, but I don't think he would have put so much into the whirlwind with you unless there was something else there at the start...on his part."

"He might have been infatuated, I suppose." That was as far as Clairy would go, because in analyzing it, she couldn't see that there had been more than that from Jared.

"Or maybe he just loved you as much as he was capable of loving anything outside of what he did," Quinn suggested.

"You think that's how it was with my father," Clairy returned.

"I do. Because I don't think Mac *didn't* love you. I think he just loved you as much as he could love anything or anyone other than the marines. Maybe it was the same with this guy and his work."

"Then I'd say that I need someone who can love me more than that," she said.

"I'd say you deserve that," Quinn said quietly.

And there they were, both of them at junctures in their lives that left the future up in the air. Clairy newly divorced, armed with a lesson and resolutions but no assurance what would happen from here, and

Quinn undecided about where to let his own personal life go.

But to Clairy it seemed as if they'd arrived at a moment in time, a place, that felt like a haven, suspended between their pasts and the futures that hadn't yet begun. And it was as if what had been happening between them since Quinn had arrived in town was coming awake once more in his cobalt blue eyes scanning her face, peering into her eyes, his focus solely on her...

All thoughts of the past really did fade away now.

Quinn raised a palm high on the back of her head and leaned in far enough to kiss her forehead—a kiss that consoled, that said everything was going to be all right, better.

Then, just when Clairy thought he would go on to a more potent kiss, he took his hand back, sat straight and put distance between them.

In a voice that was slightly gravelly, he said, "It's dangerous for me to stay, so I should probably take off."

Take off your shirt...take off your pants...

"You're afraid of me?" Clairy challenged.

"Yep," he answered without a qualm. "Afraid of how much you make me want you. Afraid of what I might do about it."

"Because you'd rather not?"

"Oh, I'd rather," he said emphatically. "But last night—"

"Was last night and tonight is tonight…"

She hadn't thought this through. She hadn't made a decision. So why was she flirting with finishing what they'd started the previous evening? Flirting with him?

It was because she wanted him.

Still, she reminded herself that it was Quinn who had ended things—even if she might have somehow conveyed hesitation, he'd been the one to cut it short.

"*But last night* what?" she asked, repeating what he'd said before she'd interrupted him.

"Last night I was on the verge of no return and I didn't want to do anything rash. And that's still true."

"Except that now we've lived with the idea for twenty-four hours…" she pointed out in a temptress's tone she hadn't planned.

"So it wouldn't be rash?"

Everything in her was crying out for exactly that— being rash and impulsive and just giving in to what her own body was demanding of her.

But she couldn't bring herself to admit that out loud, so she answered only with a smile and a small shrug of one shoulder.

Quinn turned his head partially to the side and gave her a suspicious glance out of the corner of his eye. "Where're we going with this, Clairy?" he asked, insisting on candor.

"Upstairs?"

"Don't make it my call because I'll say yes." Another warning. "So be sure," he commanded.

She cocked her head and studied him, considering it all before giving another flippant remark.

Marabeth had advised her to just have fun for this one night. It was an alluring idea.

But it would be with Quinn Camden. The jaw-droppingly handsome Quinn Camden, who was *that kind of man* that she was so determined to avoid. That kind of man her father had been. That kind of man Jared had been.

Tonight Quinn wasn't that kind of man, though. And he hadn't been that kind of man since he'd shown up in Merritt last weekend. Since then—and tonight—he'd been attentive, interested in her, not at all self-involved or distracted by anything. He'd been agreeable, understanding, cooperative, caring and compassionate.

And even if he went back to being the kind of man she wasn't going to get involved with again, a single night wasn't involvement. It was just phase one of her postdivorce life. Nothing serious. Just fun...

As long as she made sure that she *did* come away from it unaffected and detached...

Could she do that? she asked herself.

After her divorce, after her father's death, after all she and Quinn had just talked about tonight, she was craving something less serious as much as she was craving him. And Marabeth's idea of just doing this for fun suddenly seemed like the best advice anyone had ever given her. So she swore to herself that she would make absolutely certain not to read anything more into it than it was, and she honestly thought she *could* keep herself from getting attached.

"Upstairs," she decreed.

Quinn laughed. "That sounded like an order. I'm good at taking orders. I'm good at giving them. But I don't think that's how I want this to go…"

"How do you want it to go?"

He smiled a sexy smile and looked into her eyes again as if there was no one else on earth. Then he replaced his hand on the back of her head to hold her to a second kiss, this one an enticing meeting of their mouths—a light, lips-parted, sweetly sensual kiss that didn't say *upstairs* at all.

It said *relax and let me do the work…*

Which was a relief to Clairy on this first foray out of a lengthy relationship that had been void of any intimate inspiration and left her a bit unsure of herself.

But not unsure of what she wanted, so she parted her lips more, beckoning his tongue to come and play.

There was no tentativeness in Quinn's answer—he instigated a game of cat and mouse that Clairy eagerly joined as her hands rose to the back of his neck, up into his coarse hair, then down again to those splendidly wide shoulders.

With one hand still cradling her head, his other

arm came around her to pull her in closer, and Clairy's palms glided down to lie flat against his back as their kiss deepened.

There was something about kissing him that was so natural that it was almost as if he was the only man she was ever meant to kiss and she'd finally found him.

But the minute that thought came to her, she curbed it, telling herself it was not one-night-stand thinking and could put her in jeopardy.

Besides, that kiss was too good not to merely enjoy on its own merit. At least for a while longer.

Until it began to occur to her that she'd never seen him shirtless and that brought back her inclination to relocate.

She didn't know if he sensed that, or if he just had the same inclination, but he looked into her eyes again.

"Still sure?" he asked.

"Still sure," she said in a whispery tone she'd never heard herself use.

Then she took the initiative, and his hand, stood and pulled him to his feet to take him into the house, through the kitchen and up the stairs to her room, where she'd left her small bedside lamp on to come home to tonight.

But now, standing beside the bed, she wasn't so sure that had been the best choice—even the faint glow of the single bulb seemed too bright to her when she thought about shedding her own clothes.

So she bent over and turned off the lamp.

When she returned to looking up at Quinn, she found a knowing smile on that handsome face that she could still see fairly well in the bright glow of moonlight coming in the bedroom's windows. But he didn't say anything. He merely kissed her again, chastely, as if taking a cue from her need for the modesty of darkness.

It didn't matter, though. Even a virtuous kiss was still a kiss, and now that they actually were upstairs, in her bedroom, containing what was between them was impossible for more than a fleeting moment.

Quinn had no problem finding the zipper of her dress, lowering it slowly.

That was all the encouragement Clairy needed. She rolled up the bottom of his shirt, breaking away from the kiss long enough to take it off over his head.

She couldn't sneak the peek she wanted, but it did give her free access to his bare back. From expansive shoulders down to his narrow waist, up his sides and forward to pecs, where the discovery of his tight male nibs made her own nipples kernel even tighter in answer.

Quinn had an agenda, too. Clasping his strong hands around both of her arms, he brought her up against him before those hands burrowed inside her dress's opening to her back.

Thick, adept fingers manipulated her muscles, loosening them, ridding them of tension at the same time he aroused her and made her itch for even more.

Then those hands went up to her shoulders, snaked under the straps and coasted downward. Her dress dropped to hang on her forearms, leaving her breasts uncovered.

A brush of cooler air turned her nipples diamond-hard and Clairy let the dress fall from her wrists to the floor around her feet, leaving her only in her lace bikinis…and feeling a bit bolder.

Bold enough that when she reached out to him again it was to the waistband of his jeans.

There was a substantial greeting waiting there behind his zipper, and Quinn helped set it free even as he disposed of his shoes.

With mouths and tongues still engaged in the kiss that was purely erotic by then, Clairy felt him take something from his pocket to drop onto the night-stand before he shrugged out of everything he was wearing.

Which meant that he was there, right in front of her, in her bedroom, stark naked.

And she just had to look.

She evaded the kiss, returned to tug at his bottom lip with her teeth as a promise of more, but then went to the limit of his arms in an effort to see him.

He didn't let her. He leaned forward to recapture

her lips instead, bending her far back before he eased her onto the mattress with the escort of that kiss.

She was alone on the bed with only his hands on either side of her as he continued pillaging her mouth with his for a few minutes, teasing her.

But in a short while, he ended that kiss and stood tall and glorious.

Intent on removing her bikinis, he seemed unaware of what he was presenting for her to see. But Clairy used the opportunity to finally have that glimpse of his body that she'd been after.

It was worth the wait and she devoured the sight of a man more magnificent than any clothes had done justice to—he was lean, amazingly muscled and endowed enough to take her breath away.

Once her underwear was gone, he paused to take an appreciative look at her that actually added to that endowment before he got on the bed beside her.

He was on his side and she turned to hers, too, peering into that excruciatingly handsome face of his, into those blue, blue eyes.

But what they'd begun couldn't be denied and everything was unleashed then.

Mouths collided once more as Quinn held her in one arm while his other hand reclaimed her breasts and brought newly delicious torment.

Sometimes light and feathery, sometimes strong and firm, sometimes his whole hand pressing her flesh and then just gentle fingers tracing contours, circling her nipples, gently pinching…

Clairy nearly shuddered with excitement, thinking that it couldn't get any better. Then he replaced his hand with his mouth and taught her how wrong she'd been. So much better that her shoulders lifted off the mattress in search of even more.

She ran her own hands over every inch of him, striving to cause a similar reaction in him, but the stalwart marine was rock-solid under even her most tantalizing caress.

Until she reached low enough to encase that lengthy staff of steel and brought a quick arch of his spine that let her know she had just as much power over him as he had over her.

So much that it drove him away, searching for the protection and pausing only to use it.

Then he came back with even more intensity, more hunger—to her mouth again, to her breasts with even more raw, wicked passion, to spots she hadn't even realized were sensitive or could make her writhe.

And when she wasn't sure she could keep herself from the brink, he found a home between her thighs.

His caution returned once he was there, though, moving into her oh-so-carefully as he kissed her with a contained hunger.

She tightened herself around him and raised her hips.

It was the only signal he needed, as he began to

move with divine deliberation, in and out at first, at a pace she learned and matched. Then more quickly. More quickly still, until they established a rhythm that became so organic Clairy could just let it happen and concentrate on what it was creating in her.

Every thrust, every retreat, served a purpose, increasing the pleasure, taking her further into it, and further still until she crossed into so much more. Into a burst that carried her with it, higher and higher, to a culmination that stole her breath and held her in its grip as every nerve ending glittered in the most incredible climax she'd ever had.

And as he plunged deeply into her to find his own crest, another intense wave of pleasure swept her up and held her atop yet another peak that she hadn't known she could ever reach. Only when it, too, passed did Clairy realize her fingers were digging into his back. She let up on him and wilted into the mattress again, welcoming the weight of him as his strength drained away.

For a few minutes, that was how they remained, breathing heavily, hearts pounding hard against each other.

Then Quinn took a breath that pushed his chest even more firmly to hers, sighed into her hair and rose up onto his elbows to give her a kiss that was nothing less than a profound confirmation of the connection they'd made that seemed one of more than mere bodies.

"I don't know what to say," he whispered with awe. "I didn't know it could be like that…"

He looked confused, but she understood because it had never been like that for her, either.

She could only arch her eyebrows and nod.

"Can I stay the night?" he asked.

It wasn't easy for her to rise out of her own awe, but she worked at it, managing a bit of glibness to camouflage it. "A sleepover?"

"I wasn't thinking about letting you get much sleep."

Clairy smiled. "Okay."

He laughed. "After a breather," he added, pulsing inside of her as a teaser of what the rest of the night would bring before he slipped out of her to escape to the bathroom for a brief moment.

Then he was there again, beside her on the bed, on his back, his arm under her to scoop her into his side so closely her leg went over his massive thigh.

He grasped it and tucked it higher, more securely to him.

"You're okay, right?" he asked, his voice thick with fatigue.

"I am" was all Clairy had the energy to answer.

"And after a ten-minute snooze?"

"I'm not going anywhere," she joked, amazing herself by how much she wanted him again already.

"Thank God," he muttered as his entire body relaxed—all but his arm around her and his hand on her leg, both of them keeping her right where he wanted her.

And as Clairy also gave in to the need for rest, she was a little worried.

Because she just couldn't be sure if anything she did could keep her unaffected and detached...

Chapter Eight

A ridge of steep, densely forested mountains formed the western border of Merritt. After a punishing workout at the gym on Saturday, Quinn hit the most rugged trail through the roughest terrain to the top of one of them for an equally punishing run.

It mimicked a day Mac had designed for him at the start of his freshman year of high school. The only difference was that when Quinn reached the flat top, he stopped. For Mac, the training exercise was only complete when Quinn made it back down again within the assigned time, without a pause to rest.

But today he did pause to look out at the view of Merritt below, scanning it until he located the general vicinity of Clairy's house.

After his night with her, the workout wasn't actually the way he would have chosen to spend Saturday. He'd wanted to spend it in bed with her.

But she'd had plans. She'd already made a date with Marabeth to go to Billings, where Marabeth would shop for a wedding dress and ask a cousin to be a bridesmaid.

So after making love for the fourth time at dawn, Quinn had reluctantly let Clairy out of his arms to get ready for her day trip and he'd gone home.

It had been his intention to go home to sleep, but when he'd plopped down on his own bed, sleep hadn't come as easily as it had in Clairy's bed, with Clairy curled up next to him.

Instead, for some reason, he'd started hearing Mac's voice in his head, taunting him and keeping him awake until he gave up trying and put himself through one of his mentor's specially designed drills.

The drill Mac had demanded of him the day after Mac had caught him showing off for Nicole Parisi, and Quinn had confessed that he liked her and was thinking about asking her to his first homecoming dance.

"You want to be a ladies' man or you want to be a marine?" Mac had shouted. "Females are a distraction—either show me you're serious or don't waste any more of my time!"

Quinn had finished that training two minutes under what Mac had allotted, and he hadn't asked

Nicole Parisi to homecoming—he'd used that evening for another of the workouts Mac assigned him.

In fact, after that, whether Mac had been around to see it or not, Quinn hadn't gone to a single school dance all the way through high school. He'd cultivated a few friendships-with-benefits that had given him a way to lose his virginity and gain some experience, but that was it. He'd been determined not to be distracted, to become a marine, and to continue to prove to Mac that he was serious about it.

"But here's the thing, Mac," he said into the quiet of the deserted mountaintop, as if his mentor was there with him. "All those years ago, this workout was enough to get Nicole Parisi out of my system. Today it didn't do anything to make me stop thinking about Clairy."

Or wanting her even more than before they'd had last night together.

Or wanting to be with her in a way he'd never wanted to be with anyone.

Between the mess with Laine and then learning what Mac was doing to women marines, he'd been left questioning so many things. But today it seemed as if everything was coming to a head. With Clairy at the center of it.

"You gave her up for the marines, Mac. You even put making me a marine before her. But she was your kid, your family, and you just blew her off…"

Not that he had any room to judge when he'd

done the same thing to Rachel, to Laine, Quinn told himself.

But while Rachel and Laine had given him some small look into the way his actions affected them, listening to Clairy talk about what it had been like for her with Mac as her father had really opened his eyes to how wounding Mac's behavior—and his own—had been.

"You were important to me, you know, you old hard-ass," he said affectionately. "I wanted to be just like you. I've devoted my life to it. But when it comes to the kind of life you actually had, the kind I'm headed for…"

Quinn had no idea what his mentor's relationship with Clairy's mother had been like. But since Quinn had become an adult and more of an equal to Mac, he did know what Mac's private life had involved.

Mac hadn't had *relationships* with women. He'd had women he slept with. But that was the extent of it—satisfying physical need with women who didn't want anything more than that themselves.

And if ever one of those women changed their minds, it went one of two ways—if a woman wanted more, she never heard from Mac again. If a woman cut him off, he couldn't have cared less because he had no attachment to any one of them—he just bided his time until someone else came along.

"And after Laine, that's what I was figuring I was

probably going to do, too, to keep any woman from getting in too deep with me."

But now?

Now he'd had a taste of more...

So much more, with Clairy...

What he'd found with Clairy wasn't what he'd had with Rachel or Laine or any of the other women over the years. Looking back now, he knew that they hadn't sparked in him what Clairy had.

He'd enjoyed slightly more of the female companionship than Mac ever had—dinners and dating, meeting friends or sometimes families, some small amount of cohabitating. But he'd still never invested anything of himself.

And if he went on doing that—doing even less than he'd been doing and following more of Mac's example—he was going to end up with even less than his mentor. No wife or kids. No nothing except the marines.

Certainly no Clairy.

When considering what path to take to avoid the kinds of things that had happened with Rachel and Laine, going Mac's route had seemed like it might be the best way. But thinking about it now—knowing that it meant no Clairy—was a hard pill to swallow.

"Did you have any idea how great she is?" he asked his lost mentor. "Because she *is* great. She's... everything."

That was what Tanner had said when Quinn had

been attempting to understand his brother's resignation from the marines—he had said that Addie was *everything* to him.

At the time, Clairy had inexplicably come to mind, but still Quinn hadn't been able to see his brother's point of view. Now he was beginning to.

He'd never been a big talker, and yet when he was with her, words flowed. It seemed important that he tell her whatever he was thinking, that she see what he was about, that she know him.

That had never mattered before. In fact, he'd guarded against letting anyone get to know him too well, against being too transparent. He'd always played his cards close to the vest.

And he'd actually listened to every word she'd said. Listened, paid attention, recalled, been eager to hear more.

He knew that no other woman he'd ever been with would believe *that*, but it was true.

He wanted to know what was on Clairy's mind, how she viewed things, what made her tick. He wanted to hear her stories, her opinions, her interpretation of things. He cared what she thought. He liked the back-and-forth with her. Liked that she could admit when she was wrong, but that she held her ground when she wasn't, that she didn't retreat.

And something strange happened to him when he was around her—when she came into a room, or the minute he caught sight of her, even if there were other people around, things inside him just settled, relaxed, seemed right.

When he was with her he felt somehow stronger, more capable, more complete. He found comfort in her, he thought, as he recalled that she'd helped him deal with the guilt he'd felt over that last fight he'd had with Mac before the heart attack. And support, too, when he'd confessed his decision to put a stop to what Mac had been doing, despite the fact that it meant going against the man he'd never felt anything but loyalty to.

"And damn if I couldn't look at that face forever..." And run his fingers through that red hair, search those green eyes. And smooth the backs of his fingers over that satiny skin.

He ached for her all over again and his hands itched just to touch her.

Everything...

His brother's sentiment echoed in his head again, and with it came the certainty that that was what Clairy was to him—everything...

Everything he'd never known he wanted. That he wanted so much now he could barely stand it. So much that something old stirred in him—the drive, the determination to have her at all cost. At any cost. The long-ago single-mindedness that his mother had instilled in him, that Mac had honed, not to let anything stand in the way of having her, of making her his own, of never—ever—letting her go...

Which meant what? he asked himself.

Offering her his military life? The kind of life she'd grown up with?

He knew she wouldn't agree to that. And it wasn't what he wanted to give her. It wasn't what she deserved. Especially not from him.

Plus, it wasn't what he wanted with her, he realized suddenly. He wanted that *more* that they'd been having since he'd arrived in Merritt. He wanted to be an ever-present part of her life. He wanted a *full* life with her, without the gaps that living a military life would cause for them both.

He wanted to be *everything* to her, too.

And if they had kids—which, as odd as it seemed to him, he discovered he could actually picture—he sure as hell didn't want to be to them what Mac had been to Clairy.

"The thing is, Mac," he said now, "I *do* know how great Clairy is. And I don't want to miss a minute with her. You may have loved her as much as you could love anything or anyone other than the marines, but for me it's different."

As sure of that as Quinn was in this moment, he knew what he had to do to have her.

And although it shocked him right to the core, he realized suddenly that he was willing to do it…

Well, *that* was a sight to come home to! Clairy thought as she pulled into her driveway late Saturday evening.

After a long drive from Billings and dropping off Marabeth at Brad's house, she'd been eager to get home and fall into bed to catch up on some of the lost sleep of the previous night with Quinn.

They hadn't made plans for tonight and it was after eleven, so she definitely didn't expect to see him standing on her porch when she drove up to her house. But there he was, leaning with one tight T-shirted shoulder against the post, all but his thumbs slung in his jean pockets, that sexy stubble on that too-hot-to-believe face.

One look at him wiped away her fatigue and left her thinking about falling into bed with him again, sleep be damned.

After all, he won't be here forever. Even if I spend more than a single night with him, why not enjoy this while it lasts?

Because it wouldn't last long before his leave ended. Which meant that even if sleeping with him became a multiple-night stand, she had no illusions about it being more than a temporary tryst.

I can live with that, she told herself as she began to take off Quinn's clothes in her mind.

"Fancy meeting you here," she said, flirting when she got out of the car.

He smiled the devilish smile she'd seen so much of last night and she thought that confirmed the reason he was there.

But as she approached the house, the wicked smile

turned into one that was more controlled as he said, "I just came to talk."

She didn't believe it, but she pretended to. "Okay. We do that pretty well, too."

"I'm serious," he said, pushing off the post to stand straight and strong—a force to be reckoned with.

"Okay," she repeated, suspending her fantasy of undressing him, since a rerun of the previous evening didn't seem to be immediately on the horizon. She also braced herself slightly, thinking that he could have come to tell her that he *was* leaving even though his ten days weren't over yet—that was something her father had done.

"Come in," she invited, going to the front door.

By the time she'd unlocked it, he was behind her, holding the screen open.

"How was your day in Billings?" he asked as they went inside.

"Productive—Marabeth found two dresses. The bridal shop is going to hold them for her for a while so she can make up her mind. Of course, the one she really likes costs about four times as much as the other one. We looked at bridesmaids' dresses— ugh… We had a nice late dinner with her cousin, who's excited to be a bridesmaid, and then we drove home." Clairy set down her purse and they moved into the living room, where she turned on the lamp on the end table. "How was your day?"

"Tried to go home and sleep, couldn't, got up and

did Mac's get-the-girl-out-of-my-system workout that's followed by a run up to Mason's Peak," he answered.

Get-the-girl-out-of-his-system workout? Am I the girl? Does he want me out of his system?

Instinctively, Clairy took refuge in the self-protective mode she'd learned as a child to help deal with her father's attitude toward her and his ever-looming departures.

She didn't ask Quinn to sit and didn't sit herself. Instead, she stood behind the easy chair at the opposite end of the room, gripping the back of it. "And now here you are to tell me you got the girl out of your system," she declared.

Quinn shook his head slowly and let out a small chuckle. "Not hardly," he muttered more to himself than to her.

"But you came to tell me something. That you're cutting your leave short?"

"Not that, either. The exact opposite—"

"That you're going to stay longer?"

"Forever—if you'll have me."

"Come on…" she cajoled, thinking that he was joking but not quite getting the joke.

"I mean it," he said, moving to the arm of the sofa nearest the easy chair she was using as a shield. He dropped onto it, his thick thighs spread, his hands clasped between them.

Seeming more relaxed than she felt, he went on.

"You know your dad was my idol and five months ago I sort of watched that idol crumble. It left me with a lot to think about. A lot about the way I've thought of and treated women myself, about how they did—or didn't—fit into my life. It's been weird," he said with the air of someone who had finally worked things out for himself.

"I was starting to figure I needed to just do what Mac did," Quinn went on. "I was thinking that playing at having relationships where I had one foot out the door didn't amount to treating women any better than he had, so I should probably just skip relationships altogether, find women who wouldn't get in any deeper than I did, and give my all to the marines without any regard to anything else, the same way I basically always have. Then our paths crossed, yours and mine…"

He paused, gave her a soft smile and explained all he'd thought about during his workout, during a rest before he ran down Mason's Peak.

"The thing is, Clairy," he said once he'd told her everything that had gone through his mind, "since I was a kid, I wanted to be what your father was. But I realized that maybe that isn't true anymore. He wasn't the man I thought he was. There were some big flaws that I was blind to. But now that I've seen them…" Quinn shook his head. "Those aren't footsteps I want to follow in, and I think I'm back to looking at following in my father's, in Micah's and Tanner's—I've served, I've made my contribution, and now maybe it's time to come home…"

He paused again for just a moment before he stood and moved to the back of the easy chair, where she was, where she had to turn to face him.

Looking into her eyes, he said in a soft voice, "I've been the marine I've wanted to be. But you make me a better man, Clairy. You make me more the man I want to be now. And being with you, making a life with you, having a family with you, is the future I want. I love you."

Oh, those three little words…

Initially it stunned her to hear Quinn say them. To hear him say them with so much sincerity that they rang as deeply true. The words sent goose bumps over the surface of her skin, made her pulse race and excitement wash through her.

Until she recalled another time when those words had swept her off her feet. When Jared had said them.

And she also recalled that she'd sworn never again to let them override her common sense or her better judgment.

She closed her eyes, forced herself to be rational, reasonable and analytical, rather than emotional. And only when she thought she had a tight grip on those things did she open them again.

"*Maybe* you don't want to be like my father. You *think* you want to follow in your father's and your brothers' footsteps. *Maybe* it's time to come home," she said, reiterating his own words, mounting an argument. "*Maybe* and you *think* equals you're not sure, you have doubts."

"I had doubts as I headed up Mason's Peak. I didn't have them by the time I came down."

It was Clairy's turn to shake her head. "I don't trust that," she said flatly.

"You don't trust me?"

"You were a little bitty boy when you came here, so sure of what you wanted to be, what you wanted from my father, and that has *never* wavered—"

"Until five months ago."

"When it wavered even more toward being who my father was and only making women recreational. But before that, before you had your faith shaken, for all these years, for what amounts to nearly your entire life, you only *ever* wanted the life my father had, to be the marine my father was to his dying day."

"I admit that," Quinn acknowledged.

"And that's it? Boom! All of that, a lifetime's goal, a lifetime of work, and it's over? It's done?"

"It's changed," he insisted.

"It's taken a hit. For now. But—"

"And you think what?" he asked. "That I'm trying to suck you in like your ex did with that flashy whirlwind courtship? That I'm trying to get you to say you love me, too, that you'll marry me, have my kids, but ultimately I won't come through for you any more than that other guy did? Any more than Mac ever did? You think I'll decide to stay a marine and you'll be stuck in the same boat you grew up in and then married into, too? That you'll just be *incidental* to me?" he said, repeating her own description of what she'd been to both men.

"Yes," she said with a staunch raise of her chin and no question in her voice.

Quinn nodded calmly, patiently, not at all like her father would have in the face of being denied something he was putting himself on the line for.

Then he said, "I understand that you're afraid of a future, or having kids with someone like your ex or Mac, with someone whose career is more important to them than you are. And you're right—that has been me. But that isn't how I want the rest of my life to be. I *don't* want the rest of my life to be the way Mac lived his. Marabeth believes Brad grew up, grew out of who he was before—just give me that much and let me take it from there."

"If Marabeth is wrong—"

"She isn't. Just give me the same chance, Clairy! I know now how much I took away from you when we were kids—let me spend the rest of my life giving back to you. Giving you what you deserve, not only because you deserve it, but because I love you with my whole heart, my whole being. And I *want* you to have what you deserve. Because I love you as much as it's humanly possible to love anyone. And I want to spend the rest of my life proving it to you. I want to spend the rest of my life *with* you, by your side, with you by my side. I *don't* want to sweep you off your feet—I want both of your feet planted firmly on the ground right beside mine."

"My feet *are* firmly planted on the ground." So firmly that she couldn't help remembering the awful teenager he'd been and fearing that that might have carried over somewhere in the man, that even if it wasn't obvious now, it could still be lurking behind the scenes to reemerge, the way Jared's obsession with work had.

Her feet were planted so firmly on the ground that regardless of how sweet his words were now, she couldn't let go of the memory of how hard Quinn had worked to become what he'd wanted to be, to become the marine her father was.

So firmly that she couldn't take the step Marabeth was taking.

She shook her head a second time, stubbornly. "I won't take the risk, Quinn. I didn't really know who Jared was until after I married him. But I *do* know who you are. I know what you've put into becoming who you are. I know what you've always wanted. And it's all the more reason I can't believe you can just say *never mind* and change."

"Not even for what we've had since I got to town? Not even to have what we *could* have?"

A third, even more resolute headshake.

Quinn stared at her as if he couldn't believe what

he was seeing, what he was hearing. But she resisted seeing what was just before her in that handsome face filled with raw emotion. Instead, she saw him as the image of her father, as the image Quinn had striven for. She saw the die-hard marine. She saw another man devoted to something she could ultimately never compete with.

"You can't deny how good we are together," he said, daring her.

"Or how bad it was when we were kids, or how bad it was for me with my father, or how bad it was with Jared," she countered.

"It won't be any of that from here!" he said, frustration raising his voice.

"I won't take that risk," she said so definitively there was nothing else to be said. "You should go," she urged.

"Clairy—"

"I mean it. You should go!" she said in a louder voice of her own, because as much as she believed all that had just made her decision for her, she could still feel the soft spot she had for him and she didn't know how much longer her will to resist him could last.

"Don't do this. Don't let what's nothing but water under the bridge cost us both everything we could have together."

For a moment, Quinn went on looking into her eyes as if he still couldn't grasp that she was shutting him out.

So she raised her chin even higher to confirm that she was, and said in a voice she'd intended to be forceful but that instead came out with painful determination, "Go."

Quinn did another round of headshakes. Took a deep breath and exhaled in frustration that was now tinged with what she thought was anger.

"I've always meant what I said—when I said I wanted to be a marine, I did what I had to do to be a marine. What I'm saying now is that if you'll have me, I want to be here, with you, for you. I want to be your husband, father to your kids, until we're two ancient, wrinkled white-hairs who die together in our sleep."

What she took from that was that if she wouldn't have him, he would go back to his original course, back to his career in the marines. Back to what he'd always wanted to be and seen himself as.

So it wasn't as if he was committed to ending his career.

If a different kind of life was what he genuinely wanted, wouldn't he be doing it with or without her?

One more time she shook her head in refusal, then said, "Go now."

For a long moment, he stared at her, and Clairy met those blue eyes, fighting the thought that he was giving her the opportunity to stare into them forever, to have the sight of that staggeringly handsome face with her day in and day out.

Why did you have to come to talk tonight? Why didn't you just come to take me upstairs again so we could have had at least one more night together...

"Go," she said so softly it was almost inaudible. She felt her willpower slipping and needed him to be anywhere but there when she couldn't hang on to it any longer.

She saw his jaw clench. But this time he didn't say anything. He just turned and left her safely behind her chair.

She tried not to, but couldn't help turning enough to watch those broad shoulders as he aimed for the door.

And maybe that was when her willpower snapped altogether.

Because in that instant, something happened to Clairy. Something that took her away from the part of her that saw how handsome he was, how sexy he was. Something that wasn't connected to that urge to be back in bed with him.

It was something completely different that came over her as it registered that he really was doing what she'd told him multiple times to do—he was leaving.

But it was *Quinn* who was leaving—not the little boy who'd stolen her father's attention. Not the teenager she'd hated. Not the marine fashioned after her father. Not Jared.

Quinn.

Quinn, who had absorbed the worst of her resentment toward him, repeatedly apologized and bent over backward to make it up to her rather than striking out, the way he could have. Quinn, who Mim had said wasn't altogether responsible for Clairy's lack of a relationship with her father and been right.

Quinn, who had so gently shown her more clearly who her father had been and in the process taken away the burden of thinking she'd somehow failed as a daughter.

Quinn, who had redeemed himself, worked himself out of the hole he'd been in with her—the bad blood, the obstacles, the ugly history—and made her feel things for him that she'd never felt before for anyone.

Quinn, who had done that by listening to her, by showing an interest in what she had to say. Quinn, who had been suffering his own grief, his own letdown by her father, and had still been understanding of her.

Quinn, who had just told her that he meant what he said.

That was her father through and through. The General had always said what he meant and meant what he said.

If that was true of Quinn…

Was she taking the wrong thing from what he'd just told her? Should she have taken from it that when he said he was ready not to be a marine anymore, to make a life with her, that was as true for him now as his determination to be a marine had been for him before?

He wasn't indecisive—that was the last thing that could be said about him from the time they were small children. He knew his mind. He knew what he wanted.

And tonight he'd been telling her that *she* was what he wanted.

A life with her. A family.

And she was too afraid to believe it...

He reached the front door and raised a hand to the frame of the screen door to push it open.

He was leaving and he'd be gone and this would all be over.

And she wouldn't have him.

"Wait..." she whispered.

He stopped. Hand still against the screen, he turned only his head to look at her over his shoulder.

"It's all happened so fast, faster even than with Jared," she whispered again.

"We've known each other since we were kids," Quinn reminded her.

So while what had happened between them might have had an even shorter timeline than she'd had with Jared, there weren't likely to be any surprises. If she could accept that Quinn was ready to stop being a marine and start being devoted to her alone...

"What would you do if you resign?" she asked tentatively.

"I like the idea of helping vets the way you do," he answered with no hesitation, no question, clearly having thought it through. "I was hoping I could go to work with you for Mac's foundation."

He removed his hand from the door and turned to face her again from that distance. "I also like the idea of coming home to Merritt, being with my brothers again, with Big Ben. Being here if he needs me now and as he gets older."

"When is your contract up?" Clairy asked, knowing that after so many years in the service, his commission was continued by way of contracts.

"About five weeks. But I have more accumulated leave that I could take to run it out."

So he didn't have an obligation that would take him back for months, when he might decide to stay after all.

"I just… How could being a marine be as important as it's always been to you and now just… change?" she asked.

"Looking at Mac through a clear lens started it. It went further while I was questioning myself, realizing that I had two choices—to have Mac's life or the life I can see having with you. Last night, feeling the way being with you felt—the way *I* felt— and knowing when I sorted through it all today that *that* was what I want from here on…" His eyebrows arched. "I just knew. I *love* you, Clairy," he repeated even more firmly. "*Nothing* is more important than that to me now. The thought of not having you, of ending up like your dad…as nothing *but* a marine? That's the worst punishment you could give me for the things I've done to you."

It sounded so much like the truth.

And it came down to trusting that he really did mean what he said. And that he honestly had changed.

Marabeth knew Brad when he'd been a not-so-nice teenage boy, but she wasn't letting herself be held back by who he'd been in the past. She was looking at him in the present.

Should I follow in those?

There was nothing about Quinn that had ever left a doubt that he knew what he wanted. If what he wanted had changed, why *shouldn't* she believe it? Why couldn't she trust that he did know himself, know his own mind?

"There's nothing for me to punish you for," she said. "I know now that I wouldn't have had a relationship with my father even if you'd never come around—it was something in him that made him see me as less because I wasn't male."

Quinn took a few steps back into the living room. "I wasn't nice to you when I was a smart-ass teenage boy," he reminded her, as if he needed to be sure she could move beyond that.

"No, and I hope that isn't still somewhere inside you. But I haven't seen any signs of it." In fact, she'd seen the opposite in his patience, his consideration, his calm even when she'd lashed out. "So it doesn't seem like I should punish you for that, either."

"Then don't."

"You actually do see yourself not being a marine anymore?" she asked with a glimmer of hope in her voice.

"Once a marine, always a marine. But active? No. I see myself with you," he said simply.

Oh, it wasn't easy to let go of so much that protected her from more pain...

But her guard had dropped, and once it had, she knew why it wasn't just his looks and sex appeal that had made her stop him from leaving.

She loved him.

She came out from behind the chair and met him halfway. "You're sure?"

Quinn closed the rest of the space between them to stand directly in front of her again. "Of everything."

Clairy breathed a tiny laugh. "Maybe it's strange that I doubted that," she mused.

"Or maybe I earned some of it," he conceded. "Just say we can put this fresh start back on track and take it from here."

"All the way to the altar and kids and a whole life together?"

"All the way," he confirmed unfalteringly.

"I *do* love you," she said, as if she was helpless not to.

"I'm a lovable guy," he joked, making her laugh.

"You haven't always been," she chastised play-fully.

"I will be from now on, though," he vowed.

Clairy was again looking up into those eyes, that face, and this time she was brimming with what she felt for him. "I love you," she said with some awe.

"Enough to marry me? Have babies with me? Get old and cranky with me?"

"Old, maybe, but let's try to avoid cranky."

Quinn smiled that smile that only made him all the more handsome. "I'll give it my best shot," he promised as his hands cupped the sides of her face and held it for the kiss he placed softly on her lips.

The kiss that couldn't stay that way for long before all the passion of the previous night came alive again.

And as Clairy closed her eyes and indulged in it, not only could she envision a future with him, but suddenly all the pain and struggle and offenses of the past also seemed worth it if it meant she could have the man he'd become.

* * * * *

Get 4 FREE REWARDS!

We'll send you 2 FREE Books plus 2 FREE Mystery Gifts.

Harlequin Special Edition books relate to finding comfort and strength in the support of loved ones and enjoying the journey no matter what life throws your way.

FREE Value Over $20

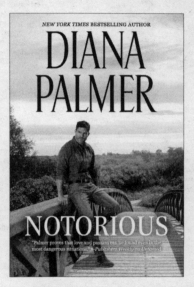